Grandmother, Grandmother, come and see

GRANDMOTHER, GRANDMOTHER, COME AND SEE

G. H. Morris

*To Harriet and Martin
with best wishes
Geo Morris
31.3.89*

Constable · London

First published in Great Britain 1989
by Constable and Company Limited
10 Orange Street, London WC2H 7EG
Copyright © 1989 G. H. Morris
Set in Linotron Palatino 11pt by
Redwood Burn Limited, Trowbridge, Wilts
Printed in Great Britain by
Redwood Burn Limited, Trowbridge, Wilts

British Library CIP data
Morris, G. H. *1939–*
Grandmother, Grandmother, come and see
I. Title
823'.914 [F]

ISBN 0 09 469010 3

To my mother

1

How my uncle Lancaster Brightside and Charlie o'
the Terrus End came back from the War

Let me tell you about my uncle Lancaster and of the day that he came home from the Great War – that was the day on which I had been made to return to school following a nasty attack of the whooping cough.

Uncle Lancaster is my father's younger brother, a twin to my uncle Albert. When they were born, Albert was so much bigger than Lancaster that their mother, Emily Brightside, thought that the one would fit quite snugly inside the other – just like Russian dolls. Consequently, during their early years my poor grandmother lived with the perpetual fear that Lancaster might one day be gobbled into the belly of his larger brother. Old Doctor Cartwright, who knew the family's pipes as well as any water engineer would have known the layout of our drains, was unable to explain such a variation in sibling size but his son, the young Doctor Cartwright who continued in the practice of his father after the old man's retirement, considered that a battle had been going on and that the larger of the twins had been stealing all the nourishment from the smaller; he named their period of gestation as the War of Emily Brightside's Womb and he wrote a paper about it which was to have been published in a distinguished medical journal. The editor's secretary, on seeing the title, however, imagined that the piece of writing was destined for a history magazine which happened to be published by the same organisation. The consequence is that the young Doctor Cartwright's observations constitute the only gynaecological tract ever to have appeared in the *Journal of World*

History. It was published complete with diagrams and bibliography and it completely mystified the historians.

Young Doctor Cartwright was unable to explain exactly what had happened but I think there was a notion that Albert had been sitting on his brother's umbilical cord, perhaps even giving it a nasty nip with his transparent embryonic fingers and causing a kind of back pressure to be built up, so diverting most of the available nourishment down his own tube. Their two volumes were soon to even up, however, when in early childhood Albert suffered a terrible illness from which he almost died and during which time Lancaster decided that it was time to inflate. Again, nobody was very sure as to what exactly had taken place, but by the time that Albert had recovered from his illness, the two were as alike as two peas. Young Doctor Cartwright saw it as an extension of the War in Emily Brightside's Womb – the weaker hitting back at the stronger, but being very careful in choosing his moment, so to speak.

By the time that I was born, early in 1913, it was almost impossible to tell them apart. By then the two brothers were both accomplished artists; Albert had already completed some of the world's most famous one hundred paintings, copied from a book which Great Great Grandmother had bought, and Lancaster had photographed several reels of kinematographic film – experimental kinema he called it. Before he had gone off to join the Flying Corps, my uncle Lancaster had been employed as the projectionist at the Royal Picture Palace in Kippax and due to the kindliness of the owner, Mr Pinkofsky, he was able to view his own experimental films during those hours in which the establishment was not being used by the general public. Albert never went to war, choosing instead to go down the pit with my father. He lived in a gaily painted wagon which was parked beneath the village gas lamp. He shared it with a French rope walker called Rosanne and they had a child called Clarrie who was a couple of years younger than myself. My grandfather, Ernest Brightside, as he bounced

8

Clarrie upon his knee said that she had a skin like porcelain. As the only other porcelain figure which I knew of was a pot spaniel which stood on our mantelshelf, it wasn't until I was about ten years old that I realised Clarrie to be human. Until then I somehow imagined her to be a dog.

Clarrie and I were struck down with whooping cough at about the same time and young Doctor Cartwright had advised our parents that we should be taken to sit by the gas works. My father and uncle Albert, each carrying a chair from around our dining table, walked the two of us into Castleford, a journey of several miles. When we arrived at the gas works there were already dozens of children sitting in the hazy sunshine forming a circle about the small gasometer. They were tied down to their chairs with white cord and each was coughing his guts up. Both Clarrie and I were admitted to the circle like children get absorbed into a game of ring o' roses except that we were unable to hold hands for we too were tied down to our chairs. Then we were left to breathe the foul air whilst our fathers went off to the pub. Clarrie started to bark and I watched her porcelain face and thought, poor little spaniel. Then I looked about me at all the other barking children and wondered which of them had skins of porcelain. Which of them are dogs, I wondered? I started to cough. The spasm was uncontrollable and the wooden dining chair jumped up and down to the sound of my coughing and with me still firmly strapped to it. The air was foul, like one of my grandfather's farts. I could hardly breathe. Then in one of those rare periods when I was able to stop the whoop I saw that everyone else was in spasm, spittle smearing their red cheeks and full wet lips. Although I'm sure that they would have wanted to weep, there was no time for crying – there was hardly time for breathing. I thought to myself as I watched their dancing chairs and bloated faces, I thought, why am I the only one out of step, so I threw myself wholeheartedly into tune and coughed my little guts up until the chair fell over with me still strapped to it. Then

Clarrie started to laugh and she was laughing and coughing so much that she too managed to tumble over her chair. The smell was now quite vile and causing some to vomit. Eventually they too toppled one by one choking in the hazy sunshine. When our fathers had returned from the pub we were mostly on the ground staring up at the sun as if it was an unexpected alien and totally exhausted from the rigours of our treatment. There was hardly a sound or a contortion from any of us; the small gasometer, a metallic sentinel, watched over us in silvery solitude. My father righted my dining chair and untying me he said to uncle Albert, 'Good stuff, this gas.' My uncle, surveying the silent children like so many dead soldiers bogging up a stinking trench in that peculiar afternoon's heat, nodded his agreement. 'Must be,' he told my father; then he untied Clarrie whose porcelain cheeks flamed as angrily as the fire in our parlour.

As I told you, by the time that uncle Lancaster came from the War I had recovered sufficiently from my illness to have returned to school. It was my first day back. I was six years old and in Standard One and my teacher's name was Wenceslas Piggott. Senseless Spiggot is what most folk called him but my great great grandmother, Jane Brightside, who had been the kindliest of women found no exception in Wenceslas and had called him the Good King, for he had educated my father and his twin brothers way beyond what might have been expected only a few years before. He was still a young man when he started upon my own education – in his early forties, I suppose – and he had a heavy black tash. The schoolroom was painted two-tone green. There was a thin brown line which had been painted half-way up the walls and which encircled the room, with a couple of breaks only for the windows. The line however did cross the door. Anything above that line was painted a pale green colour and anything below the line was painted the colour of the muddy grass of the winter common. My uncle Albert had been invited in to brighten up the place and he had painted a couple of Turners and a Constable into the walls

10

of the classroom. There was an unfinished Rubens at the back of the room. An outline of two full female bodies had started to appear and there was endless speculation amongst the children as to whether the ladies would be given their painted clothes or not. In their incomplete state it was difficult to imagine them one way or another for I had not so far laid eyes upon the naked female form and had no real image of what lay beneath a lady's heaving and bumping clothes, yet it was equally difficult for me to visualise two colliers' wives sprawled across that sumptuous bed in full black skirts, laced-up boots and shawled heads. In any event what they might be doing with each other in such a situation remained a complete mystery.

Wenceslas Piggott sat at his desk at the head of the glass facing forty noisy children and he threw a yellow rag at me.

'Come on, Donald, lad. Tha can clean this rubbish off the board,' he said referring to the words which he had chalked on to the blackboard when teaching us about gold mining in Africa. I began to clean the board and as I watched the half white words disappearing and tried to comprehend the other half white words which remained at each arced wipe, Billy o' the Terrus End who sat by the window said, 'Please sir, there's two puppets attached to a biplane in the sky.'

Mr Piggott rose up from his desk, ambled to the open window and stuck his head into daylight. Sticking one's head into daylight from the gloom of our schoolroom was not just moving it from one abstract intensity of light to another, it was more like thrusting the head from one medium to another. Like shoving it 'twixt air and strawberry jam. Schoolroom windows were a painful reminder of the other world.

'That's not puppets, son,' he said excitedly, pulling his head back into the room. 'Them's men. Men on parachutes coming down from the sky.' And he rushed back to his desk. I felt the heat of his enthusiasm as he opened up the lid close by my face. Now here is education, I thought as I continued to wipe the zebra-striped words from the blackboard, for until that day I had learned only of how to keep myself clean at all ends and how to open a door for a lady – a category which I became surprised to know included *both* the coal owner's wife and my grandmother. I'd also learned of wool and sheep and had just started to learn something of gold; unfortunately the whooping cough had deprived me of lessons in leather and silverware. But the look on Wenceslas Piggott's face as he grabbed his spy glasses from deep within the black well of his desk, and from right in front of my nose, told me that parachutes, whatever they were, were far more interesting than anything which we had tackled thus far. I needed to know about parachutes, I thought as I watched him race back to the open window. Our schoolteacher thrust his head into the day again, this time ogling through his spy glasses.

'Well, that's odd,' he said, bringing his head back in again and looking directly at me. 'They've got no bloody trousers on.' Now parachutes sounded interesting, but parachutes without trousers sounded even better. I needed to know more and ran from the schoolroom as quickly as my small legs would take me.

'Grandmother, Grandmother,' I was shouting, 'there are parachutes coming from out of the sky and they don't have any trousers on.'

'Donald, come back, lad,' the schoolteacher shouted from the open window as I whizzed along the strip of grass at the front of our school. 'Come back, Donald, where does tha think tha's off to?'

I turned my head just for a moment, sufficient to see Billy o' the Terrus End drop from the window and attempt to race after me.

'Wait, Donald. Wait for me,' he was shouting, with Mr Wenceslas Piggott hanging half out of the window to keep a firm grip on the young lad's breeches.

It was only then that I realised that I hadn't the faintest idea of what I was doing. What is a parachute? Where am I going? Why am I running from Wenceslas Piggott? What is

12

it that I wish to tell my grandmother? Is this really what education is all about? I looked into the sky. Two men were floating like thistledown. They seemed to be miles above me but I could clearly see that they were men and they floated like the seeds of a plant on a warm summer's day. Yes, I confirmed excitedly to myself, this is education; this is schooling worth having. I seemed to collect myself together and ran off with the bits gathering in my head and I was again shouting, 'Grandmother, Grandmother, come and see. Come and look. There are men like parachutes coming out of the sky and they haven't any trousers on.' With my eyes firmly on the men in the sky I ran slap bang into my grandmother who had wandered on to the common beyond our front door.

'What is it, Donald? What is it?' she asked, trying to still my shaking head held between her gentle hands.

I pointed into the sky. 'It's men, Grandmother. Men like parachutes. Mr Piggott says they haven't any trousers on.' My grandmother raised her eyes to heaven and we both watched the biplane trailing smoke and phut-phutting away to disappear behind Hunger Hill. Then we ran together to stand directly beneath the falling men. I gawped at the spidery trouserless legs above me as they fell through the dry still air. Then with a little drift sideways they started to climb again and we watched the parachutes going up into the blue.

'They're not supposed to do that.' It was Wenceslas Piggott's voice shouting behind us. He had brought out the whole class to observe like he did sometimes when we were on a nature ramble. 'I can't understand that,' he said, looking into his spy glasses.

The parachutes then continued in their descent until there was another small sideways movement and the men started to ascend again.

'They've got some peculiar undergarments on,' said the schoolteacher, tearing his eyes from the lenses. 'And they're bloody going up again.'

'Mr Piggott!' warned my grandmother heavily on hearing the teacher's bad language.

'Ay. I beg tha pardon, Mrs Brightside. But I never saw owt like this afore.' He looked through the glasses again. 'They've got knickers on. Great big knickers.'

My grandmother smiled as the men started to descend again. 'It must be Lancaster,' she told me excitedly. 'It's our Lancaster,' and she gave me a hug. They were now no more than fifty feet above our upturned faces and we saw how their large knickers seemed to billow out as, caught in the updraught, they filled with air and again shifted the trajectory of the parachutists' fall.

'They've bloody double gussets in 'em and they're made of silk I think,' I heard our schoolteacher telling the class.

'Well, they would have,' said my grandmother to the excited schoolteacher, 'and there's no need for such language,' she chastised. 'It was I who made them, tha naws, Mr Piggott. I allus let in a double gusset. An' now the War's over I can tell thee another thing,' she went on. 'I made the parachutes too.'

'Now, Mrs Brightside, there's no need for stories,' the schoolteacher advised.

'I did,' she protested but Mr Piggott wouldn't hear of it and concentrated his attention through the spy glasses and on to the billowing knickers of the ascending men. How strange, thought my grandmother, that men who saw themselves as educators had themselves so little stomach for the stuff of it, for what my grandmother had been telling him was perfectly true. For a period of three years now, she had been employed at Mr Gaylord's knicker factory which was situated just outside the village and on the road out to the next village – that's the village where we have our church. About two years back a man from the Ministry had paid a top secret visit to Mr Gaylord and the factory had been commissioned to make parachutes to a stolen German design. Mr Gaylord had said that it was essential war work and Emily Brightside had been entrusted, along with two

14

other women, to cut out and stitch up the silken canopies on a special machine that had been pinched and shipped out very daringly from right under German noses at a factory in Berlin.

Now, not only was my grandmother an excellent seamstress, but she was also a designer with a most economical turn of mind. 'Waste not, want not' was her motto. So when she found a way of cutting out the silk and at the same time saving an extra piece of material she thought it only right that the offcut should be put to good use and so she ran up a pair of French knickers with double gusset. She saw to it that each parachute pack when folded away also included a pair of knickers for the airman – after all, someone was paying for the silk, so why shouldn't our brave lads have the use of it? That's why she was so certain that one of the two men falling out of our sky was her son Lancaster and she was able to make a pretty good guess that the other body dangling now almost to the ground was that of Charlie o' the Terrus End whose brother Billy was my classmate in Standard One. After all, she argued, Charlie was the only other village boy who had joined the Flying Corps. Wouldn't he be surprised to know that Mrs Brightside had made his knickers for him?

It had been an educated guess, she thought, still observing our village educator playing around with his spy glasses and wondering when he was going to teach the children something of that at which they gawped. But the view in the sky was an education in itself, really. One didn't need the comments of a schoolmaster. Wenceslas Piggott was defunct in such a situation and he probably knew it. As I had thought before even leaving the classroom – parachutes were likely to be educative. So much of an education, in fact, that even before my grandmother had mentioned his name, I knew that one of the two falling men was my uncle Lancaster. I had hardly any recollection of the man at all yet from the mythology constructed within the Brightside home I had reasoned that if a man was to fall

15

from the sky then it would be Lancaster. It was Lancaster who had donned the flying suits of uncle Elyahou Tsiblitz and crashed to the ground on a number of occasions. It had been Lancaster who had taken the balloon ride from London together with Great Great Grandmother and who had been tipped arse over tip to the ground, with the balloon hovering only feet above the hedgerows near our home. It had been Lancaster, the pioneer of aerial photography, who had taken film of our villagers roaming about the sky like lost planets and dressed in the strangest of costumes – everything from pterodon to pig. If a man was to fall from the heavens, then why shouldn't it be my uncle Lancaster?

My grandmother had first to find him among the billowing silkiness and when he had uncoupled his harness she hugged him. She cuddled and loved him for her Lancaster had come out of the sky without trousers and displaying the jap silk knickers which she had run up and double-stitched for the entire squadron. The trouserless hero stood in the middle of our common kissed by his adoring mother and surrounded by schoolchildren. Charlie, to avoid the same treatment, quickly gathered up Billy o' the Terrus End as if he had been a dropped parcel and ran off with him to find Mrs Terrus End. Mr Wenceslas Piggott, spy glasses strapped about his neck and with drops of sweat on the ends of his heavy black tash, at last turned his attention to the education of the children in his care.

'What happened to tha trousers?' he asked my uncle plain enough for all to hear.

'Our aeroplane was stolen,' Lancaster said sheepishly.

'Gerraway. Tha's 'avin' me on, Lancaster. How does anyone come to steal an aeroplane?'

'We was just sitting there, me and Charlie. Sitting in a field near Lincoln and talking about coming home when this man climbs on to the wing, pokes a revolver at us and tells us to take off our trousers.'

'What sort of man?' asked the educator.

16

'He was a foreigner. A German, I should think. Perhaps he doesn't realise that the War is over, maybe he intends to fly back to Germany in our biplane. He was very pleasant but very firm and he kept on poking the gun at us. He'd obviously been listening to our conversation, because he asked us where home happened to be and when we told him he said he knew the place very well and told me to take the machine home. I think that perhaps he was some kind of spy. Once we were in the air he flung out our trousers, they're somewhere in Doncaster I think.' He seemed aggrieved that his trousers were in Doncaster. 'Then when we got here he had us bale out and took the controls himself. He's no fool, an accomplished aviator I should say.'

'Ay up,' said Mr Piggott with his glasses pointing towards Hunger Hill. ''E's bloody comin' back again.'

We tipped our gaze to the sky and saw the smoke and heard the little phut-phut as the engine almost stalled directly above our heads. Then a large object was hurtling down towards us.

'Come on, gerrout a road,' the schoolteacher advised as we all turned and fled from the falling object. It was falling so fast that we thought it was going to make a large crater in the centre of our common, so it was with great surprise that, when a safe distance from the thing, we turned just in time to see it hit the ground, bounce about twenty feet into the air and bounce again this time to a height of only about ten feet. It bounced and bobbled about for a few moments and then came to a complete standstill without causing so much as a dent in the grass. It looked peculiarly like an armchair and we approached it with caution.

'Careful,' said Mr Piggott, 'it might be a bomb.'

It *was* an armchair and my grandmother, the excitement of the day catching up with her, threw caution to the wind and sat in it. It didn't explode. She said that it was the most comfortable seat which she ever had the pleasure to sit upon for it was made completely of a bouncy rubbery material which seemed to flow and mould itself to the body.

17

There was a note attached to the back of the object and it was addressed to the Brightside family. My grandmother read it whilst the biplane phut-phutted in a circle above. She then waved her arm at the aviator who waved back, or so we were told by Mr Piggott, who had caught the foreigner in his spy glasses.

'It's from your uncle Elyahou Tsiblitz. He says that the armchair is his latest invention and that your aunt Henrietta is well and has made a complete recovery from her madness.'

'Uncle Elyahou Tsiblitz!' Lancaster exclaimed.

'Uncle Elyahou Tsiblitz?' I chorused. That was the second piece of Brightside mythology to be introduced to my eager young ears in no time at all and I stared longingly after the aviator and the machine which was disappearing once more behind the dark slopes of Hunger Hill. 'Education,' I thought, watching the final lingerings of the smoke in the blue sky.

'Elyahou Tsiblitz,' said all of Standard One in an astonished tone, recalling their own versions of village mythology.

'Tha didn't recognise him?' Emily asked her son.

'No, Mother.'

'Lancaster. Tha's taken pictures of the man's bottom and tha didn't recognise him?'

'Be fair, Mother. He had on his goggles and a flying cap. How was I to know who he was?'

'Ay, but he weren't wearin' 'em on his backside.'

'No, Mother, but he had his trousers on.'

'Unlike some,' she said and then she sighed. 'E' tha's a great puddin', Lancaster. Come on, let's get some tea.'

We walked off between the walls of my aunt Henrietta's yellow laboratory, a rough stone structure which she had tacked on to the front of our house during the final phases of her madness. I looked back to see that Standard One was being given a lesson in physical exercises; seeing how far each child could bounce off the rubber chair. Most of the children seemed to catapult off it to a height of about twenty feet but Wenceslas Piggott, his black tash drooping in the heat of the afternoon, shot off to at least double that distance and landed in a pile of horse muck – then he took the class back to the schoolhouse, brushing down his dark waistcoat with limp-wristed hands and explaining that perhaps it was more important for them to learn about gold.

My grandmother led us into the house and she filled the kettle with water from our tap in the scullery and brought the kettle back into the parlour and placed it on the roaring fire.

'Where shall I sleep, Mother?' Lancaster asked.

'Tha'll sleep down 'ere in Sidall Junkin's wide winged chair. Mr Brown's in t'other one. The one that Bill Pettit used to have. Did tha know that Bill Pettit were dead?'

Lancaster shook his head. 'I suppose some of us had to go,' he said.

Emily thrust her hands deep into her pinafore pocket as she sat by the fire. 'Maybe,' she said, looking into the coals. 'I miss Sidall Junkin spittin' on the coals, tha naws.' She was talking of an old miner who had dossed in our parlour for years and who had died when he choked on his new set of teeth. 'Tha father and myself are in the room above like we allus was. William and Mary and little Donald are in tha great grandmother's old room at the front here. Tha naws she's gone too, does thee?'

'Ay, I heard something of it.'

'Ay. I went up to bathe 'er one day and all the green had gone from her skin. All the black, all that coal dust had gone too and she had the skin of an angel, white as Christmas buttons, and she suddenly opened her eyes and she smiled at me like she were a babe, like she smiled at thee when tha was born, Lancaster, and I thought it were all going round in a big circle and she just passed away the next minute while I was bathing her face and I were thinking how it all comes around in a big circle.'

Lancaster's lip trembled for an instant and I thought that he was about to cry. Then he said, 'Where's my camera, Mother?'

'It's under her bed,' she said. 'Tha camera's safe enough.'

My grandmother mashed the tea then she said to me, 'Go get Rosanne and Clarrie, love. Tell 'em that Lancaster's come 'ome.' Then to Lancaster she said, 'Albert's still with Rosanne in the wagon – they've a little girl now, Clarrie they call 'er.'

'Goodness,' I thought, 'today must be a very special day for my grandmother is making tea and having visits out of turn.' For unlike when my great great grandmother was alive and had run the house, Emily had a time for everything. Our parlour was a dining-room and a kitchen and a bakery and a playroom and a bathroom, a study and an artist's studio, and when the old woman had been alive it had been a laboratory and a pharmacy too and more importantly it had been all those things at one and the same time. While some had eaten, the children had played beneath the table, Henrietta had baked and Albert had painted, old Jane had made her potions and the world had passed in a mad whirl of activity. Just like it did in the Terrus End house where me and Billy played under the table whilst the rest of his large family got on with whatever it was they had to do. But Billy played in our house only at playtime – half past four till five and never beneath the table. Then the props were changed and new actors were shoved in to get on with the next activity – baking till six. Then it was bath time and the water was poured into the tin tub. Then it was meal time. Then it was time to read or study and possibly time for a little idle chatter before it was bedtime and the lodgers flew off on their dreams in the wide winged chairs like demented voyagers in the fairy stories sail away on the backs of the flying swans. Emily, unlike Jane, had got it organised and what an extraordinary display of precision clockwork it was. But today, because of the return of her son, she was letting time scramble itself –

whatever would the neighbours say, Rosanne was to visit and it was still the cooking time. Tea would be taken in the kitchen and not in the dayroom.

'Mother, I'll not take tea,' Lancaster said moodily and he suddenly stood up. 'I'll just go and pack up the parachute.'

'No tea, son? Why ever not?'

'Don't fuss, Mother. I'll be happier packing up the parachute.'

'Is something wrong, Lancaster?'

'No. I don't think so, it's just that I never returned home from a war before.'

'Not since tha was born anyroad,' his mother answered him. 'Go on then, son. Pack up tha things. Tha'll see Rosanne and Clarrie later.'

My uncle went back to the common where Charlie, alone, had already started to pack away his parachute. The two didn't talk, they seemed to be each one stuck with the memories of his jerking and silent family like a film running in his head. Lancaster walked around his parachute straightening out a billow of silk here and a knotted cord there. Then I watched him folding it ever so slowly, and ever so carefully away. Bit by bit, segment by silken segment the parachutes disappeared into their packages and the two aviators, without so much as a glance at one another, carried them off to their respective homes.

'Tha can get Rosanne and Clarrie now,' my grandmother told me as she was putting away the baking trays – the tin tubs would be out soon, steaming before the roaring fire. Visitors at bathtime, I thought. Crikey, even old Jane Brightside wouldn't have allowed visitors at bathtime. I fetched them from the wagon, holding my cousin's hand all the way. She was still whooping and her porcelain cheeks were all aflame. Rosanne gave Lancaster a big kiss upon his forehead and told him that she was pleased to see him home. Then, as Clarrie and I played beneath the table, the three adults chatted about Lancaster's adventures in the Flying Corps and eventually I heard them leaving the house as they went outside to greet the menfolk coming home from the pit. The two of us still beneath the table, I showed the neatly packed parachute to Clarrie and she tugged at a corner of silken white which peeped invitingly from within. It immediately doubled to two corners of silken white. Then just as quickly doubled again to four. The canopy seemed to have a life of its own and as Clarrie undid a button and I tried cramming back a full billow of silk, a second wave of material found its way into the room. I imagined that this was how a many-headed monster might behave when the knight had lopped off a head. I was telling the material to get back into the canvas pack but Clarrie had now undone another button and there seemed to be no room left beneath my grandmother's dining table.

I scampered out from under and stood up. I tried rolling the segments as I had seen my uncle doing but I only succeeded in bringing more of the soft material into the room. Clarrie was completely hidden beneath the canopy but even worse she had the still mostly buttoned up pack with her. I was painfully aware that there were still many more buttons to be undone. The amount of free material suddenly doubled in size. It undulated to the window. I tried kicking it back beneath the table but only succeeded this time in getting it to mount half-way up the stairs. I heard Clarrie coughing and then being sick. She was vomiting in my uncle's parachute. Then there was a sudden draught and the white folds opened a little. The silk had blown into the scullery and a little had crept to the top of the stairs. Clarrie, completely unseen, was undoing more buttons. In fact by this time I couldn't really see anything other than the billowing silk which floated about me in a quiet diffused light. I remember hoping that the door to my father's bedroom would be closed and then from somewhere came the answer that it wasn't for I heard my father's voice asking, 'Whatever's that at bedroom winder?'

Then there were noisy footsteps and angry voices raising the wind and, unfortunately, the canopy too. The parachute blew itself more deeply into my family's little home. Water was being chucked on to the fire and I heard the sizzling of the wet coals and they spoke to me like many things in our village would speak to a six-year-old but the coals were talking through a silken muffle of whiteness and I hoped it might be God telling me that this wasn't my fault. I could hear other children's voices and whoops of laughter. People were running up our steps to the bedrooms and Albert was shouting for Clarrie.

'She's under the table,' I managed to say.

'What bloody table?' came back my uncle's response and I decided that it might have been more prudent for me to have kept my mouth shut for in raising my voice I realised that I had given my position away. I was yanked up into the air though still completely surrounded by billowing silk and passed through a window. Moving from the diffused light and into the bright blue day made me blink. Then suddenly I was on the grass next to Clarrie and surrounded by adults all shouting at me.

'What's a think tha's bin playin' at?' my father asked.

'Leave the lad alone,' my grandmother said. 'He doesn't understand.'

Not understand, I thought. Whatever does she think it is that I don't understand? I wanted to tell her that parachutes were pure education – now I knew all there was to know about the bloody things. They brought men from the sky, they nestled into small homes. I understood everything.

'Well, there's no watter and there's no fire and the house is full of parachute,' my father said, glaring at Mr Brown, our lodger, 'so there'll be no baths, not for any of us,' and he fetched me one around the ear. Then my father turned to the house with such a disbelieving look on his face. Billy o' the Terrus End had just slid down a piece of canopy which was pushing its way from our bedroom window and which had almost found its way to the ground. The parachute, working from the inside, was now beginning to wrap itself about the outside of the house. Here was more education.

23

This was mathematics at its most interesting. Parachutes could both wrap around and themselves be wrapped up at one and the same time. Here was the geometry of surfaces at its most baffling best – a topological nightmare. Billy was quickly followed down the slide by Danny Pratt and he by little Jackie Henderson. My father was gobstruck as he watched the three of them re-entering the house, finding their way blindly to our rickety stairs and obviously preparing for a second go.

'Where's tha think tha's going?' asked my father, trying to find his way into the house once more but being beaten back by the flapping of the silk. Emily collapsed to the ground, clutching at her side with the pain of laughter. Ernest and Albert had to support one another for fear of falling in their merriment and Mr Brown had eventually to come to their rescue by supporting the pair of them until eventually all three tumbled over. The neighbours too, who had all come to watch the antics in our house, sank to their knees in fits of the giggles. Eventually Lancaster's dam burst too as the sepia memories ran momentarily from his head and he saw my father trying to do battle with no more than a posh woman's frock. 'My parachute's done for,' he told his mother with tears of laughter streaming down his cheeks.

His mother looked at him for what seemed to be a full minute hardly able to control the speech which she wished to deliver over the tide of laughter which broke at her tongue. Then very quietly and with a control that could push back waves she said, 'No matter, Lancaster love. I'll be able to make dozens of pairs of French knickers for all the little lads in t'village.'

2

The Bellman, the Schoolman and the fire brigade

Ah'll tell thee a riddle.
  Ay. Tell me.
  I'm tellin' thee. I'm tellin'. Listen. What is it that binds the Bellman, the schoolteacher and the lads in t'fire brigade?
  Nobody was speaking. They were just disembodied voices. In our village sometimes you could hear the stranded voices. There was a voice in the winding wheel as it cycled endlessly through the drizzle. There was another in the metal-tasting rain which spattered the roof of the terrace. And yet another which spoke from the cold stone in the walls of our house. Aunt Henrietta had known that voice. A sad melancholic voice in the old stone which spoke to her of its history – that was an unhappy voice which in its turn created madness. But these were neutral voices speaking to me now. The tones were soft and clear like someone telling a story to the hushed children sitting cross-legged on the floor in Standard One.
  'I don't know,' I said aloud and my mother stirred in her sleep. I had my small hands gripped about the silken crook of her arm as she slept. She faced my father clothed in his fancy striped pyjamas; her back to me. The collar of her rough nightdress scratched at my face as she turned from a disturbed dream.
  Doesn't tha know? Doesn't tha know what gives 'em a voice? 'No.' That was my voice again. 'What's tha riddle?'
  I'll tell thee, shall I? Shall I tell thee?
  'Ay, tell,' and my mother shifted again making me move away from her to avoid being suffocated beneath the beached body tossed up from her dream.

It's bell, lad. They all share the same bell.

'Oh yes, the bell,' I said. 'They all have the same bell.'

'Shh, Donald,' said my mother. 'Go back to sleep, son,' and she put her arm about me.

The Bellman is a sort of town crier, except that in a village like ours he doesn't need such a big voice and he doesn't shout *Oyez* or *Hear ye* or anything like that. He just says *Sithee* in an ordinary quiet way and he rings his bell in the rain; then he tells you things. Things about other people or about other villages. During the War he had stood in the rain dressed in his oilskin cape and his black fisherman's hat. He has a silken white beard which hugs the lines on his face and he told us what was happening in the War. How many had been killed or who from the surrounding villages and pits had died or been maimed. Things like that.

Our Bellman is called Jacky Jellis and he has an old dog called Bruno. My father had known Bruno when he had been courting my mother, that's how ancient the dog is. He's called Bruno only when he's with the Bellman, but when he plays cricket with the lads on the common he's called Percy Holmes and can catch a cork ball in his mouth. I always feel so sorry for Bruno. He has no teeth, but that isn't the reason why I feel sorry for him. Not exactly. I feel sorry for Bruno because he has such intelligent eyes. Bruno is so intelligent that he actually knows that he's a dog, that's why I feel sorry for him. All the other dogs in our village don't know the difference between a dog and next Thursday, but Bruno does and it creases me up that I know that he knows. You see, if Bruno knows that he's a dog, then Bruno knows that I'm human and he can see the difference and I'm sure that Bruno would like to be human too, just like me. He looks at me with his sad brown eyes and I know that he's asking why he can't be just like me and why he has to walk about on all fours and catch cork balls in his toothless mouth. Why he can't eat at table instead of scavenging about with all those other dogs looking for scraps of food.

'I don't know, Bruno,' and I give a little whimper and my

26

mother tightens her arm about me in her sleep and I wish that I could turn a key and unlock the human in Bruno. Release him from his canine imprisonment, either that or I wish that somebody would take him away so that I didn't have to see his intelligent sad eyes any more.

The bell is kept in a little wooden box on the outside wall between the two windows of our schoolroom. Wenceslas Piggott sometimes rings the bell to call us to school on a morning or after the break for dinner and Marlene Jellis, the Bellman's daughter, who teaches Standard Two rings it to call an end to lessons. She sometimes calls us to school too, as does Miss Fountaine, the headmistress. Marlene Jellis has long ginger hair which she can sit on but she ties it in a bun at the back of her head and my grandmother says that she's a loose woman and that she is having an affair with Mr Piggott. She says that Marlene goes into the pub with him and unlike the other women she doesn't sit in the snug but she sits in the bar with the menfolk and drinks with them and listens to their foul language and that's no way for a schoolmistress to behave. She's a loose woman? But her hair is scraped back in this bun with not a strand out of place. Perhaps she's only loose when she is sitting on her hair, when her red hair falls over her face and touches her bottom and all over.

'Perhaps that's when she's loose,' I murmur and my mother edges closer to me and away from my snoring father and his fancy pyjamas. I turn my head to avoid the roughness of her garment again.

When there is a fire anyone can ring the bell and the fire brigade come running with their buckets of water and their ladder; when the Bellman comes he just carries the bell off with him, clanking it and shouting *Sithee* until somebody has the time or the inclination to hear what he has to say. Then he returns the bell to its little wooden box in the wall and walks off to the next village to tell them things. Things about us. I suppose that he's already told them about my uncle Lancaster and Charlie o' the Terrus End coming out of the sky and about how wicked Clarrie and I were when we undid the parachute.

It weren't tha fault.

'I'm sorry.'

'Shh. Go back to sleep, Donald,' says my mother. 'God's already forgiven thee.'

Wenceslas Piggott was a bachelor, his mother and father were both no longer alive and because he wasn't a pitman himself he never had colliers lodging with him. He lived alone and ate his breakfast alone. He never knew what it was like to live in our village, not to truly live with others in our village. The jam in his sandwich was making his tash tacky and he ran his tongue over it tasting the sweet sticky edge of hair. He gulped from his mug washing the hot tea back on to his lips to dissolve the strawberry jam which had stuck there and his tash dripped tea on to the tablecloth. He heard the ringing of the school bell, picked a book that he would need from his bookshelf and dashed from the house which was just around the corner from the school. Actually, everybody's house was just around the corner from the school, it was just that Mr Piggott lived nearer to the corner than most. He said good morning to Mr Clayton, the caretaker, who stood in the yard. Mr Clayton was thin and wiry like a piece of ivy in a waistcoat and a flat cap. The schoolteacher went into his classroom and sat at his desk. He put his head in his hands and with elbows resting on his desk he stared at the wall at the back of the classroom, wondering when our Albert would complete the Rubens and whether the ladies might get some clothes. Then he looked at the forty empty desks before him. The school bell rang again.

'Oh, Christ,' he said without shifting his hands from his head. 'It's Saturday.' He rose up slowly and walked out of the school and into the small yard. Mr Clayton was ringing the bell.

'What is it, Mr Clayton?'

'There's a fire, Mr Piggott,' the caretaker answered, removing his flat cap and scratching at his balding head.

'A fire?'

'Yes, Mr Piggott. You can see the smoke on't terrace by t'common,' and he pointed a nicotine-stained finger towards our house.

'Yes. Oh, yes Mr Clayton. Right,' said the schoolteacher, following the direction of the accusatory finger. 'I'll do summat about it, right away,' and he went back into the school to get his spy glasses.

'Shouldn't tha be gettin' t'others?' Mr Clayton shouted at him from outside and rapping at the closed window.

'Yes, Mr Clayton. Right away,' Piggott shouted back through the dirty glass whilst strapping the glasses about his neck.

There was a team of six local fire fighters. Mr Piggott, Mr Hardwick the owner of the pub and Charlie Gill our next-door neighbour who had been invalided out of the army – they formed one half of the team. The other half were all colliers and because it was Saturday morning Wenceslas Piggott knew that they would be down the pit. He ran to the pub and hammered on the door turning his spy glasses every once in a while on to our terrace. A wisp of smoke came from one of the downstairs windows.

I could hear the tap-tappings from way below ground. The men were at work and there were disembodied voices there too.

Why isn't tha father in t'pit, this mornin'?

He's in 'is striped pyjamas.

And what of Mr Brown, the inventor of brown paper? He's not shouted up the steps yet.

He must be off to somewhere in his wide winged chair.

Where Donald where? The question was tapped hard into the dark shining coal.

'China,' I said.

And tha grandfather? Where's tha grandfather?

'My grandfather's bent in two, almost clapped out from tapping tha two foot seam, tha bastard.'

Tha grandfather must go to work, Donald.

'We had a party for my uncle Lancaster coming from the War and we had beer and Scotch whisky to celebrate his homecoming. That was unusual because my grandfather normally won't allow alcohol into our house.'

He's temperance tha naws and like Winston Churchill he's been brung up to have the utmost contempt for people who get drunk.

'I saw them curl and pack away the ripped parachute, even the bit with Clarrie's vomit on it. Then they went and got ale and whisky from the pub and they all got drunk, all except my grandfather and my grandmother. Nobody had a bath and they all went to bed when it was light outside and the dawn was touching at their black faces.' I opened my eyes and looked upon my mother's sooty face. I glanced across at my father's blackened face too. The sun's rays streamed through the window.

I could hear Charlie Gill at the other side of the bricked-up hole in our bedroom. He was making a strange noise like he was being sick whilst hopping about on his one leg. The Bellman seemed to know that Charlie had only one leg even before Charlie himself knew it. One day he had stood there with Bruno sitting on his foot, the rain was lashing at his cape and he was making his proclamation. He seemed to be so ancient that the Gods had to hold him up with strings like a celestial puppet who they kept on sending back down to talk with us. *Sithee*, he said and rang the bell. It was like the fanfare which heralds the coming of the narrator in a play.

He introduced the one-legged Charlie Gill who hadn't yet come home, but Jacky Jellis knew all about Charlie's other leg – the Bellman knew where it was. It's funny how the narrators always know what's going on. I don't know why they bother to have scenes and acts and all those actors when all that's needed is a good narrator who can remember the story. Perhaps that's the reason, perhaps they can't always rely on the narrator to get it right and they need the actors to nudge his memory. Perhaps that's what actors are – just scraps of memory in the narrator's head. Perhaps that's why the narrator only appears on odd occasions – the rest of the time he's thinking and all those actors are only a playing-out of his wild thoughts. So Charlie came home as Jacky Jellis told he would and he went to live with his mother. There was no more rugby, no more fooling about. Life was for real now. Now that the stinking war was over for him and they'd grabbed his leg from him, life was for real. And Charlie couldn't face too much of that reality so he started to drink – drink more then he used to do, that is – and Charlie bloated up like a balloon so that his one leg couldn't support the massive gut which he had and he kept on falling over. I could hear him vomiting up my grandfather's beer and his Scotch whisky whilst trying to stand on his one leg.

'Poor Charlie.'

'It's too early, Donald, go back to sleep.'

There's smoke, can tha see the smoke?

Ay.

Can tha smell it? Can tha smell?

'I can smell smoke, Mother.'

Wenceslas Piggott was hammering at the door of the pub. 'Wake up, Rube Hardwick,' he was shouting. 'There's a fire.'

Rube put his head out of the upstairs window. 'What's up, Mr Piggott?' he asked, scratching at his vest.

'There's a fire, Rube,' said the schoolmaster and he pointed in the direction of our house.

'Ay. I can see t'smoke,' Rube said as he looked over at our terrace. 'I'll be down soon. I'll meet thee over yon.'

Wenceslas ran aimlessly back towards the schoolhouse where Mr Clayton was still ringing the bell.

'Why don't tha get buckets?' the caretaker asked as our schoolmaster went by.

'Ay, that's a good idea. Right,' and he turned and went back into the school to get the buckets from the cupboard in which they were kept. He reappeared moments later without the buckets. 'Where's the key?' he asked Mr Clayton.

'Charlie Gill's got key, Mr Piggott.' He removed his cap and scratched his balding head again.

'Right,' said Mr Piggott, racing off to the Gill house. When he got there he was surprised to find that it was the very house from which the smoke poured.

'Charlie, Charlie Gill, is thee up?'

Charlie was hopping about on his one leg, groaning.

'Mrs Gill. Ay up, Mrs Gill.'

'Go back to sleep, lad,' my mother murmured.

'Mother, I can smell smoke.'

'What's that smell?' It was my father in his striped pyjamas sitting up in bed. 'Come on gerrup everybody.'

'Charlie. Mrs Gill. For God's sake rouse thasens.' That's Mr Piggott's voice.

My father was thrusting a leg madly into his trousers and hopping about just like Charlie Gill would do. 'Mother, Father, gerrup,' he shouted.

'Oh, my God, is it our house?' my mother shouted. 'Come on, Donald, don't just lie there. Get up.'

'Charlie, 'as tha got the key to the bucket cupboard?'

'It's next door. There's smoke pouring from the window at Mrs Gill's.' It was Mr Brown's voice calling up the rickety stairs.

I can still hear Charlie hopping about on his one leg and vomiting in his room behind the bricks, then I heard the window in our bedroom being pushed up and I heard my grandmother say, 'Never mind the buckets, Wenceslas Piggott, tha puddin'. Smash the window and get the slops,' and she rushed down the stairs with her chamber pot shouting for my father to bring ours too. I heard the smashing of the glass and the hopping of Mr Gill as he descended the stairs and by the time that I had reached the street there was a whole queue of neighbours filing in through the Gills' front door each with a potty full of pee and other stuff. Emily was orchestrating the lines and to avoid congestion she was directing people through the house and out of the back scullery door. Wenceslas Piggott sat on the grass, hearing Mr Clayton still ringing the bell, and he marvelled at my grandmother's organisational abilities. The fire was soon put out and the helpful neighbours dispersed back to their homes each having deposited his slops in Charlie Gill's parlour. If only Wenceslas Piggott had lived in our village, truly lived in our village, he would have known what was to be done.

In the area built on to the front of our house and which had become known to the family as aunt Henrietta's laboratory we kept a duck. Other folk kept pigeons and ferrets and Mr Henderson, Oliver's father, had a greyhound and a whippet. There was a whole arkful of lively animals, but we had a duck. He was just a plain ordinary duck that waddled about and swam in the water which was trapped in a cut-down rain barrel. He was far too lazy to fly though, and to get him to do something, mostly one would have to pick him up and throw him into the rain water where he would quickly settle and float about on the still surface until boredom struck. Then he would turn himself upside down and let his arse float about for a while, presumably until he became equally bored with life that road up, and then he would revert to his former position. So like some great philosophers, his day would alternate between the two worldly positions until, uncomprehending and absolutely fed up with it all, he would close his duck's eyes and go to sleep. It was whilst I was watching the duck in one of his bottom-up phases of life that Jacky Jellis rang his bell. He stood on the common in front of our house letting the rain spatter his oilskin cape, then he sat in the rubber armchair which had fallen out of the sky on the previous day and with Bruno curled at his feet he said *Sithee*. My uncle Lancaster came out of the house, grabbed me up under his arm and walked out of the walled area to face the seated Bellman. The Bellman rang the bell and said *Sithee* again but nobody else came out to listen.

'My lad Archie's come 'ome, too,' he said at last, realising an audience of two was all that he was going to get, 'but there's nowt to keep 'im here. Nowt but pit and Hunger Hill.' He looked very comfortable in the chair. 'He's one of them hintellectuals, is my Archie. He should go. Better gone and be done with it.'

'Ay. He was always the cleverest in the class, him and your Marlene. What'll he do, now he's back from the War?' my uncle asked.

'He'll be a doctor, that's what,' Jacky Jellis responded. 'I'll give 'im ten pund and he can tek the dog too and 'e'll be off to London, I expect. He'll mek 'is fortune in healing, I know that.'

'But he'll have to go to a medical school, Mr Jellis. Ten pund won't see him very far.'

'Ay, that's why he'll be taking the dog.' The rain pattered on his fisherman's hat and he roughly stroked the black dog beneath the chin. Bruno looked at me with his sad brown eyes and I said, 'I'm glad you're going, Bruno, perhaps things might be better for you in London,' and I turned my attention from the animal to concentrate on the man sitting in the armchair. He was relaxed as if nobody was holding up his old bones any more.

All the intellectuals had gone from our house too. Sidall Junkin had not been what you would have called an intellectual but he was politically aware, as was his friend, my great grandfather, James Brightside, but they'd both gone. Ernest was a church-goer, but he wasn't political. His sister, Henrietta, had been an intellectual, but her intellect

34

had been supported by madness and when the madness went I suppose her enthusiasm for things, particularly for the love of history and for the love of nature, well, they just died too. My great great grandmother, although lacking any kind of formal education, had in some ways been the most astute of all. If it hadn't been for her none of us would have survived, so she must have had a social awareness even if she couldn't turn it to political action. Even Bill Pettit had been aware, though it was only with the intelligence of a computing engine. Like the Babbage machine, Bill had been born into the wrong era. His head filled with fact had been forever breaking down beneath the weight of his knowledge. He needed some other means of storage but it hadn't even been invented yet.

But what were we left with now? After the War, what came home? Ernest was religious and Emily was organisational, but there was little intellect. Albert painted and my father worked, but they were not political. And Lancaster, who flew aeroplanes and made moving pictures with a hand-held camera, what was he?

'Mr Winston Churchill will win the day, Lancaster,' Jacky Jellis was telling him. 'Social reform won't lead to any freedoms – it will only bind us closer to the State. The State might organise us but it won't bring us owt. Authority and History are the same thing, Lancaster. They've both got big mouths and they've got to gobble to keep going, but be careful, Lancaster, because keep going they will. If nowt else History has to keep going. Be careful of them socialists, lad.'

'What are you saying, Mr Jellis?'

'I'm saying get out while tha can, lad. Go off with my Archie, piss off quick cos there's nowt 'ere for thee. Join 'em in their Empire building, lad. Theres nowt in t'pit.'

'But what'll I do, Mr Jellis? I'd be no good at doctoring or owt like that.'

'Moving pictures, lad, isn't that what's in tha bones? That and aviation. Tek the plunge, lad, and use tha gifts in the coming world. Don't be fearful of tha gifts and don't swallow all that stuff from the hot 'eads in't pits. They've seen nowt of future and they know nowt of History. They think that History is a snake whose head can be turned but it can't, I tell thee. The best tha can do is divert its head into a sack for a while, while tha teks a runnin' jump and tha hopes it hasn't seen thee. That's the best tha can hope for, understand.'

Two weeks later I saw Archie Jellis winding up the road away from our village. He had on his Sunday suit but it was a Friday and he held Bruno at the end of a piece of string and the dog was leading him over by the big house to the crossroads. That was a place where the world began, the crossroads – you could go anywhere from there, anywhere in the whole world, yet it was amazing how often people came sliding back down the hill unsure of what lay down the paths of the other three roads. Archie didn't come back, though. He and Bruno just kept on going down one of those roads.

There was the smell of creosote coming from next door as Mrs Gill was painting the floor in their parlour. She put her nose to the window and watched Archie climbing away. Then I caught sight of Lancaster with his head pressed to the window in our parlour and he too was watching the Bellman's son leaving with the dog. Lancaster shut his eyes. When he opened them again, Archie had gone.

I saw Charlie Gill hopping on his one leg and leaning on his wooden crutch. He had dragged the urine-soaked pegged rug from out of the house and on to the common. Then his mother came outside and poured turpentine on to the smelly old rug and Charlie lit a Swan Vesta and hobbled away as the flames erupted with a whoosh. The bell rang immediately. Since the morning of that fire in the Gills' living-room, observers had been posted everywhere. Within moments the fire had been extinguished by a brigade of men drilled to perfection by a smarting Wenceslas

Piggott. Charlie gave a short cry like I've seen the other invalids sometimes make and he hobbled away, not looking at anyone, until his mother went to fetch him from the far side of the common and she led him into the house. Wenceslas Piggott stood on the grass apologising to the closed door as Mrs Gill drew the black curtains over the window in their living-room, just like she used to do for the rugby team when they came to her house for a bath after the match. But I don't suppose that Charlie would have wanted to be reminded of that.

Lancaster, incorporeal behind the window in our house, suddenly materialised himself on the common. He walked down by Bottom Boat, by that part of the river where his aunt Henrietta had first descried the stones with which she had eventually built her laboratory. He brushed the aerial spiders from his face and, with his airman's head thrust back, he watched the lapwings passing over. By the river bank there was frog spawn and caddis-worm and he saw the chasing sticklebacks. He wandered into Kippax. At the Royal Picture Palace he asked Mr Pinkofsky if he could have his old job back.

'It's nice to see you back, Lancaster. It's good to see you, boy,' said the proprietor.

'How about the job, Mr Pinkofsky?'

'Are you still making those wonderful pictures?'

'I've not been back for long. I haven't had the camera out yet.'

'Such an eye. You've such a wonderful eye, Lancaster. You must take your pictures.'

'What about the job, the projectionist's job? Can I have it back?' He heard the farrier next door hammering his metal. The noise rang uselessly throughout the empty cinema.

'There's someone else, Lancaster. You didn't expect me to wait for four years, did you?'

Lancaster looked away from the owner's wrinkled-up face and contemplated the upturned orange boxes which passed for the seating for most of the would-be audience.

'She's a nice girl, Lancaster. Come tonight, come. I'll see what we can arrange. Maybe we can organise something even if it's only part time.'

'Thanks, Mr Pinkofsky.'

'That's all right. You're a good boy, Lancaster. You come back tonight, we'll see what we can arrange.' He squeezed my uncle's arm.

3

Mr Brown, the inventor of brown paper

It is often said that the Great War changed everything which it touched. Well, it didn't change our village. It changed the people all right – some of them, like those it butchered at the Somme. Bill Pettit and Oliver Henderson, they got changed in that way. It altered my uncle Lancaster. He had always been a distant child, my grandmother said, but the War seemed to have gifted him with a vagueness which was even beyond her fathoming. It blinded some and it created a lot of cripples, too, like Charlie Gill who lived next door and Mr Doyle who kept the pigs. Mr Doyle came home with only one arm and he couldn't cut up his bacon any more. But the pit could do that too, the pit could change you in those ways too. The War changed Danny Pratt's father as well; made him so he couldn't breathe. I saw him every day shuffling slowly off to the pub and gasping at every step. But the pit could even reproduce that effect in men. Who needed wars?

As I already told you, Henrietta had gone from my family – she'd not been killed or anything, she'd just run off with Elyahou Tsiblitz. He'd fought with the Germans. My great great grandmother had died and Mrs Henderson, Oliver's mother, had gone in her sleep. The other Gill boys had taken themselves off to the colonies and old Thwaite, the coal owner, had died in an armchair at the big house. My maternal grandfather, Joseph Thwaite, was now our land-lord, but he wanted nothing to do with the likes of us. But you expect with all that dying, the geography of the living changes about you, you expect that. Even the massive shire horse which had pulled the wagon on to the village common, bringing Rosanne to our Albert, even he'd been put in the pit with the ponies but the darkness had scared him and he'd galloped off into the galleries making a hell of a clatter and nobody ever saw him again.

As I say, you expect the living to change but the thing which failed to change in those years was the village itself, all the inanimate stuff. The Jam Sahib's motor car remained parked at the side of aunt Henrietta's laboratory and my father cleaned it regularly and kept it in good running order and he regularly took the crippled and the daft off to the dales in it, just like he used to do. Hunger Hill still brooded at one end of the village and the big house with its sad trees still guarded the other. In our house, the bible remained shut at the centre of the sideboard beneath the rickety stairs, emphatically closed with a large brass clasp like the golden brooch on her dress locked away Marlene Jellis's lumpy body. The bookshelf had the same few books leaning one on the other and they were still mostly unread. Aunt Henrietta's volumes, the natural history which she had written whilst at Bottom Boat, had, however, disappeared. From the window, one could still see the gas lamp but the gas company had never brought the gas into our homes and we still read and ate at night by the light of the candle. The remnants of my great great grandmother's dispensary of bottled herbal remedies collected dust and cobwebs on the shelving in the scullery and the view of the ashpits from the scullery window remained very much the same. Sidall Junkin had gone, Bill Pettit had gone too and now it was Mr Brown who raked out the earth closet each morning and tipped the contents of the ash bucket on to the smelly heap. I suppose Mr Brown was the only thing which had really changed. The War brought Mr Brown to us. It took others away but it brought us Mr Brown.

Mr Brown described himself variously to me as the inventor of brown sauce, brown chocolate and brown paper. I knew that brown sauce came only from Hammonds' sauce works and I wasn't taken in by his claim on the chocolate either, because I had already learned that it came from the Rowntree factory in York, a place where they had a church as large as a battleship, my grandfather said. On the question of his claim to brown paper, however, I was unsure, or more accurately I felt that he might have had a claim on the invention of brown paper bags. He had thousands of them, thousands and thousands. He would suddenly produce a brown paper bag from his trouser pocket or from his waistcoat and he would blow into it and then with a rising excitement I would watch wide-eyed and full of smiles; at the appropriate moment I would blink, just as he banged the extended bag between his large hands. And in that twinkling of an eye the paper bag would be no more and I would be left attentive of an empty report which he now encased in those same hands. *Wonderful, wonderful*, he would say and who was I to disbelieve him?

He was a typical dossing collier, thin and consumptive with baggy trousers and a dirty striped shirt. He had a brass collar stud at the back but he never wore a collar with that shirt; he had lively blue eyes and very unusually he had a Sunday suit. I never knew him go to church but on a Sunday he would dress up in his suit and walk about the village with a brass–topped cane in his hand and whistle the tune of one of the hymns. Or sometimes he would even go off to the next village and walk back with those who had observed the Lord, but he would never pretend that he had been to church when he hadn't. If anyone asked if he had been to church he would say, 'No. I've no time for that stuff. God and all that stuff, it gives me the pip,' but he would always make polite conversation to those with whom he walked. My grandmother thought that he looked very smart in his Sunday best and said that he was a man with a lot of pride for his suit gave him the appearance of a person with financial security. He's a man who knows how to be respectable, she said.

''Ow can 'e? 'Ow can 'e be respectable if the man won't go to church and kneel to the Lord?' my grandfather asked.

'His Sunday suit has nothing to do with God,' she told my grandfather who couldn't understand why he wore it. 'Doesn't thee understand, it's what keeps him from the poor house. His suit is the covering which keeps him from being destitute – it's his esteem. Surely tha can see that much, Ernest. It's the poor man's second skin and without it he's as helpless as a babe.' But I doubt that my grandfather could see anything of the kind.

Yes, I suppose it was Mr Brown who brought a small element of change into the village during the war years. It was those paper bags which fascinated me.

'Where's tha get all them paper bags?' I would ask.

'I telled thee, I invented 'em.'

'Tha didn't really. Not really.'

'Ay, ah did.'

'Did thee, honest? Cross tha heart and 'ope to die?'

'Ay,' and he would cross himself.

Then I would lie awake at night worrying that if he'd not told me the truth the Lord would strike him down, and when Mr Brown shouted up them stairs in the morning and I knew that he'd not been taken off in the night I'd think, well, it must be, it must be that he is the inventor of brown paper and I'd give our important lodger an extra special smile when I saw him on that day.

'I med a lotta money,' he said to me once. 'I got a penny for a dozen bags.' It was the first occasion on which I was given to consider that Mr Brown's paper bags might be worth something. In fact it was probably the first occasion on which I ever considered anything as having a monetary value. All of life is not dross, I must then have thought to myself for I suddenly had the urge to collect and save paper bags but with a definite view to one day realising their true worth and selling them on for a penny to the dozen.

'Tha must be worth a lotta money, Mr Brown,' I told him whilst imagining possession of all those paper bags.

'Ay,' he said, coughing a little and twinkling his eyes at me.

'I'll bet people believe tha's very rich.'

'Ay.'

Well, I suppose that was the small change which Mr Brown was able to bring about in me if you'll forgive the pun. But it wasn't until after the War that the inanimate things started to change and it all started on that day when my uncle Lancaster came home on his parachute. The day that the rubber armchair fell from the biplane; that, at least, changed the family's view from our living-room window. It was only brought indoors many years afterwards and it remained for the rest of my childhood, a piece of solid geometry in an alien and messy landscape.

Now I look back upon that time, it was all so obvious, wasn't it? If anyone was going to change the way things looked in our village then it would be Elyahou Tsiblitz. Look back at the mythology, look back on the reality. Either set of references would tell you – find Tsiblitz, walking, pedalling his tricycle, motoring or flying, it didn't matter, find Tsiblitz and you will get changes. Some men act as History's messengers, God knows why – I doubt if they know why themselves.

Looking beyond the village, however, beyond the deep slope of Hunger Hill which even on a sunny summer's day manages to hide its true contours in a secret shade of purple treachery, one could discern the changes which the War had ravaged. The new militancy of the working class was evident over there, beyond that hill. The War had given them a self-assertion if nothing else. There was a huge increase in trades unionism and interest in the organised labour movement and particularly among the women. Wars are sudden great explosions of power and they have the habit of awakening little eruptions, little wars in all of those involved. There had been a longing for the War to finish, for an end to come to the beastliness which mangled a loved one's body. There was an anger developed which moulded the working class from the huddled protective groups which they had been and made them into cohesive

43

forces of resistance which demonstrated a strength and a backbone. It was like God creating Adam from his clay – they became real people, upright and able to stand on their own feet without falling over. They were organising now not just against low pay and overwork but against lack of investment and poor housing and ill health and things which nobody but the capitalists had thought about before. And not merely those things; the vomit of the trenches made them wish for better things like music and books and education – somebody called it culture. But above all, the government, by asserting the social control of armaments production during the War, had shown the feasibility of the alternative to private ownership to working people. The miners wanted a nationalisation of the mines and they wanted national pay agreements too.

My grandmother ran up jap silk knickers for all the urchins of the village using Gaylord's machines. It was more or less her last act at the factory before she handed in her notice. Now that the men were home from the War she mustn't be occupying a scarce job which some man might need in order to feed his family. She believed that ours was a land fit for heroes and it was they, the lads who had returned, who would make it so.

Not many of the boys wore their knickers but the girls wore theirs and I was made to wear mine by an angry grandmother. Most of the lads ripped them up into handkerchiefs and bulged their grimy trouser pockets with them. Some cut holes about their edges and attached strings to them, turning them back into small parachutes. My grandmother wrote to Henrietta thanking her for the chair. She told her of Lancaster's homecoming and of the incident with the parachute. She also told her about the fire at the Gill house. Jacky Jellis came over and rang the bell and sat in the chair and told everyone about the contents of Emily's letter to Henrietta. It was amazing how he knew everybody's business.

44

'Archie's gone,' he then told his audience.

'Ay, we saw him leave,' said Mrs Gill.

'There were nowt for 'im here,' he told them.

'Ay, 'e was a clever lad.'

'Village is like a flower, tha naws. It's been in t'bloody bud all this time and it teks a stinking war to bring it to flower. It suddenly opens up and spits out its kids, tha naws. Spits 'em out o'er yon.' He nodded towards Hunger Hill. 'But it's for t'best.'

'Did tha hear from 'im?'

'Ay, ah heard. He walked to London and he's a place at Kink's Cross.'

'He's a railway porter, then?' Lancaster asked.

'Naw. I telled thee, Lancaster, he'll be a doctor.'

'Then what's he doing at King's Cross?'

'Studyin'. What else?'

'At King's Cross?'

'Ay, at Kink's Cross Medical School.'

'Is tha certain it's not Charing Cross, where's he's studying?'

'Oh ay. Tha's reet, Lancaster. Charink Cross Medical School. Tha wants to get thasen off, lad, afore it's too late. Remember, like I telled thee afore.'

'But how is he managing to live, Mr Jellis? It costs to go to a medical college.'

'Ay, well 'e'll live all right. 'E's resourceful lad is my Archie and 'e's got the dog.'

That was the second occasion on which I had heard Jacky Jellis mention how having Bruno would help Archie to overcome his poverty and it set in train marvellous thoughts of how the dog would earn the money whilst his master went on with his studying. Perhaps Bruno was a human being after all and once in London would slip out of his doggy skin and go off to work washing dishes in a swank restaurant. Or perhaps he would retain his doggy skin and astound packed audiences at the theatre as he recited poems and computed mathematical sums in his

45

human head. Or perhaps he would just stand in the rain with Archie, like Archie's father did, and stare at the passers-by with his sad brown eyes, and people would stare back and feel as if they wanted to cry for Bruno because he knew who he was. And they would be moved so deeply that they would put money into Archie's cap which he held in his outstretched palm. Knowing who you are like that, knowing your place like that – that must be the saddest thing in the whole world, I thought.

When Lancaster went back to see Mr Pinkofsky, the cinema owner introduced him to Mrs Cushman. She was about the same age as my uncle and her husband had not come back from the War. She didn't know for sure if he was dead because nobody had told her but he just never came home. She didn't like to call herself a widow, not until someone told her that she was.

Lancaster said hello but she was very shy and kept her eyes on the running spool in the darkness of the projection room. Mr Pinkofsky explained that my uncle had been the projectionist before she ever came to the Royal and explained a little indelicately that he had just returned from the War and needed his old job back. She had a face like a pixie and wispy brown hair which gave off the blue smoke from Mr Pinkofsky's cigarette. She sat on a little wooden chair, silhouetted in the darkness with smoke rising from her head, and said nothing. Then Lancaster said that it was all right and that he didn't need the job all that much. He told them that he could always get a job in the pit. Then she looked at him over the winding spool and the flickering images from the cinema screen reflected back on her small face and Mary Pickford and Douglas Fairbanks dazzled there, stars in her dark eyes.

'No. You have the job,' she said. 'I'll manage.'

'No, I wouldn't hear of it, missus.'

'Well, perhaps we could share the job,' she told Mr

Pinkofsky, who nodded his approval of her suggestion. 'We could work on alternate days.'

'No,' said Lancaster. 'You must have a rent to pay. You need the money for food and such. I can live at home with my mother.'

She looked away again, embarrassed by their situation.

'Well, I'll be off then,' he told them, anxious to sever himself from her awkwardness.

'You may as well watch the film,' Mr Pinkofsky said. He was disappointed that my uncle would not be working for him.

'Ay. I'll go down and watch if it's all right with you.'

Lancaster sat at the back of the cinema where there were three rows of seats of red crushed velvet. Sitting right at the back he could hear the kissing and the cuddling of the couple next to him. He'd been through a bloody war and now he had no job. He didn't know whether to take Jacky Jellis's advice and follow Archie to London. He could see that the man next to him had his hand right up the skirts of the woman he was with. She moaned softly and he wished that films had a sound to go with those talking but silent heads on the screen. Her moaning got louder and Lancaster became more embarrassed. The woman was now fumbling with the man's trouser buttons and he grunted as she revealed his erect penis. Thankfully the piano started to play. Their mouths locked together she began to masturbate the man in tune to the piano player's music. The scenes changed on the screen, the piano was played faster – a more exciting theme. The farrier next door began to bray his metal and his heavy thumpings reverberated about the cinema. Lancaster was just about to move to an empty seat at the end of the row when several people entered the auditorium and took up all of the remaining seats locking him into position beside the loving couple. He contemplated going out past the couple but decided that it probably wasn't the wisest thing to do. He continued to sit firm and thought of Mrs Cushman and her pixie face as the man next to him ejaculated to a selection of music from *Lilac Time*. The man sat back groaning for a moment as the woman buttoned up his trousers for him. Then he took a comb from his pocket and began to comb his hair watching the screen.

'What's going on?' he heard the woman whispering.

'I dunno.'

She took his hand and rubbed it on her covered breast. The screen suddenly went blank. The film had ended.

'What was all that about?' the woman asked.

'I dunno,' the man said again and put his comb away. The lights came on.

'Excuse me,' Lancaster said as he stood up. He looked at the couple. 'Oh. Hello, Mr Piggott. Hello, Marlene,' he said as he pushed his way past them. Marlene had her hair down, it was flowing past the golden brooch which pinned her together and kept her in one piece. Lancaster went back up to the projection room and sat with Mrs Cushman as she changed the spools.

'All right,' he said. 'We'll share the job, but we both work at all performances.'

'But he's not going to pay two wages, is he?' she said without looking at him.

'No. You get the wage, the full wage. I'll be all right. I'll just come in to help.'

'But why?'

'I told you, I'll manage. You need the money more than me.'

Lancaster walked home with Mrs Cushman that night after the Picture Palace had closed. She lived in Kippax and he slept the night in her bed. He was twenty-two years old and a virgin and she helped him all she knew how. He lay awake most of the night waiting for the ghost of her dead husband. Nobody came. Then he felt really dreadful because he imagined that the ghost hadn't put in an appearance simply because the man wasn't dead after all. He didn't tell that to Mrs Cushman in the morning after she kissed him on the lips and told him that he couldn't go, not until he'd done it again anyway. So he did it again then he lay on his back and felt the welcome draught blowing in at her window and fluttering up her blue curtains. They were fancy curtains, he thought, women's curtains. He watched them gently billowing in the breeze. Then he looked back to Mrs Cushman's ceiling and eventually he said, 'It can't be too difficult to make pictures talk, can it?'

Mrs Cushman didn't reply but stroked his nipple with the tip of her finger, then she wound the hair on his chest in her hand. He gazed at her pixie face and the wispy hair on her head moved in the breeze from the open window. 'I was wondering, that's all. Maybe you could record the voices as they speak and then somehow fit the film with the sound. That wouldn't be so difficult, would it?'

After a week or two he brought Mrs Cushman home and introduced her to everyone. Her name was Millie and most of us liked her. Albert didn't like her very much but my father thought that his reaction might have had something to do with the War in Emily Brightside's Womb. Lancaster never had any money but nobody knew the true reason why. His mother thought that he must have been spending it all on Mrs Cushman, which in a way he was, and she grew to dislike her because of it. She told Ernest that Lancaster was spending too much time with that married woman. Ernest corrected her, saying that Mrs Cushman was a widow woman, but Emily refused to have it, not until there was proof. It's odd how women think alike on this issue; they have to know where the other bits have got to before they can change – officially change. Men aren't like that. When Mrs Doyle went off because she couldn't stand to be living with a one-armed man and a dozen pigs any longer, Mr Doyle pronounced her dead straight away and married a young lass from the next village. Anyway, Lancaster continued to see Millie Cushman, though he didn't bring her home very often and he never had any money.

Eventually he moved in with her and they would both go

off to work together and they would come home together. Her window was always open and the cool draught always blew in her room, disturbing her curtains and swirling the dust and the soft wispy hair from her brush which she pulled out and dropped on to the linoed floor. Lancaster asked her to marry him but she couldn't do that, not without knowing what had happened to Mr Cushman. He lay awake at night thinking about pictures which talked and writing imaginary scripts for the film stars of the day. Then Mrs Cushman would wake up and make him do it and then she would turn over on her stomach and make him do it that way as well. Then one night Lancaster failed to respond. When Millie Cushman woke him up in the middle of the night and grabbed him by his soft genitals he just lay there and counted the frames in a sequence of film that ran through his head. She spread her legs and took hold of his hand and made his fingers disappear into her warm blackness but he turned his back on her and went to sleep. After that, they slept with their backs to one another every night. They went off to work together and they would come home together and they slept in the same bed but always with their backs to each other until one day Mr Cushman appeared and Lancaster came back to our house. He continued to work at the Royal but Millie Cushman moved off to another village with her husband.

4

*Aken Jugs, Owler Crimble and the latest German
fire-fighting equipment*

Throughout the next twelve months I worried about the acquisition of paper bags. If something as ordinary as one of Mr Brown's paper bags had such a value then what price should one put on my duck or on the French knickers which crept tell-tale fashion beneath the hem of my trouser leg? Through the changing school programme I pecked from Wenceslas Piggott's handfuls of education – I knew a fish from a flower and a leaf and I could name all the pink bits on the globe in the schoolroom by heart. Yet I had learned nothing of the value of possession. Indeed I had no true knowledge of the value of anything but for a brown paper bag which in my little head was costed at twelve to a penny piece.

Standard Two, if anything, proved to be even more disappointing than Standard One. Marlene Jellis spent most of her time reading from the works of H. G. Wells. She was obsessed with Wells. *The Time Machine, Doctor Moreau, The Invisible Man, The First Men in the Moon, The War of the Worlds.* She read them over and over again. Billy o' the Terrus End loved it – he knew all there was to know about aliens from strange planets. For me, however, education was proving to be a terrible disappointment. And whilst for those unlike Billy – those who didn't care much for Mr Wells' futurology – there was always the opportunity to educate oneself on Marlene Jellis's lumpy clothes or to ponder how my uncle's unfinished picture back in Standard One might look if only he could be persuaded to stroke a camel hair brush between the nooks and crannies of the female form, I thought only of the respectability conferred by possession.

We were an odd couple, then, were Billy and I. He thought only of Martians, I thought of acquisition and most of the other boys in the class dreamed of . . . Well, I was unsure of what it was which caused their world to move. However, my grandmother's analysis of Mr Brown's Sunday suit, though perhaps wasted on Ernest, was not wasted on me. Respectability was a consequence of acquisition. Collection seemed to be the only answer, but what was I to collect and from where? The answer when it came was beautifully simple and I was sure it had been sent by God. It was a coat hanger and He left it hanging in a tree.

Billy o' the Terrus End and I had skipped school one day and taken a walk down to a field called Aken Jugs – there are a lot of fields round here called Jugs. Jugs is an old word for a field and it was called Aken, I suppose, because this field was full of oak trees. We sometimes went down to Aken Jugs to collect acorns and we sometimes went just to swing on the branches or to watch the birds. It wasn't strange to find things hanging in the trees. I can remember once finding a kite all bashed up and unable to fly. Someone had left it fluttering there and knocking against the wood as the wind moved it. The kite clapped itself silly in that tree for months then one day it fell to the ground and Billy's brother picked it up and took it home; he used the string to tie up Mrs Doyle whilst he robbed the house of a side of bacon. Billy's brother's in the prison now. Another time Billy and I had found a dead fox in a tree at Aken Jugs and I said that the poor thing must have climbed up and couldn't get down, but Billy said that the cats had dragged it up there and were living off its blood. Then when we learned about lions in school I guessed that Billy had probably been right after all, and that we had a lion living just beyond the village. After that Billy and I went about with sticks for a while just in case we met the beast, but after a time we forgot about the lion and got on with our games. Anyway, on this particular day we were up in a tree and swinging on the branches when I looked across to another tree and at about my eye's level I could see a coat hanger hooked on to a small branch.

'Ay up. What's that in tree?' I said.

Billy stopped his swinging and looked across to where my nodding head was indicating.

'There's another one up there.' Billy nodded back and I followed his gaze.

'Ay, and another,' I said.

We swung ourselves to the ground and climbed the other tree to retrieve the coat hangers which hung from the branches like some strange triangular fruit. We combed the branches and as we discovered each one among the leaves we tossed it to the ground, then we came down and counted our coat hangers. We had forty-one of them and each was marked with the name of the Savoy Hotel, London W. They were lovely coat hangers, solid and shiny with varnish and polished up like my grandmother's table and the metal hooks were brand spanking new too. We looked about to see if there were more in the other trees but we couldn't find any. It seemed that there was just the one tree on which the coat hangers grew and at first we thought that we would ask Marlene Jellis how a tree could grow coat hangers, but on reflection I decided against asking Marlene anything.

'They'll only tek 'em from us,' I told Billy.

Billy gave a sigh, indicating his resigned agreement at the way in which the adult world behaved, and I told him that we would have to find somewhere to hide the coat hangers because these were going to be our acquisitions and nobody was going to take them from us. We made a pile of the hangers and covered it with leaves and grass and a few dead branches that were lying about and we set off to look for a more permanent home for our find.

There's another field close by Aken Jugs which is called Owler Crimble – Crimble because it has crooked hedges and Owler because of the elder tree which grows up from its middle like a turned–out belly button. When we approached there was a boy swinging on the gate and he had a clapper in his hand.

'Is tha clapper boy?' Billy asked him.

'Ay. My father told me to chase away sparrers.'

'Ain't no sparrers 'ere,' Billy observed.

'No. Chased 'em off,' the boy sniffed.

'What's tha name?' I asked him.

'Isaac.'

'I'm Donald and this is Billy o' the Terrus End. Hello, Isaac.'

'Hello. Is tha from t'village?' He nodded towards our village.

'Ay.'

'Ah'm from t'next village,' he told us. 'My father's got corn in this field. It's just bin drilled.' He waved his clapper in our faces and Billy stepped back, away from the raucous noise. I watched a disturbed rook flying off to Hunger Hill and we were all three silent for a moment.

'What's tha want?' Isaac asked presently. He was probably no older than Billy and I but he seemed to have the confidence of an older boy.

'Secret,' said Billy.

'What's secret?'

'What we want, daft. It's secret.'

Isaac, still on the gate, looked up at the sky and watched the clouds float by.

'What's tha do all day, Isaac?' I asked.

'Frit birds,' he answered still looking into the arched sky.

'Is that all?'

'Ay. My father says I must. I must keep birds off so I walk about whirling my wooden clapper till my arm aches or sometimes I shout at 'em. Gerron, yer bastard, I shout at the top of my voice. That scares 'em.' Another rook took off into the wash blue sky. 'Sometimes I whittle a bit of wood or sometimes I just go to sleep.' I thought of my duck

54

sleeping on the water in the rain barrel and I felt sorry for Isaac.

'Shall we tell 'im?' I asked Billy.

Billy was silent for a while, watching the stranger carefully. 'When tha falls asleep in t'crimble who wakes thee up, Isaac?' he asked after a while.

'Spiders.'

'Spiders?'

'Ay, spiders tickle me ears. That wakens us.'

Billy looked at me. 'Ay, we'll tell 'im, Donald,' he said. For some reason the spiders had made up his mind for him. For me it was the duck, for Billy it was spiders.

'We're looking for somewhere to keep us coat hangers,' Billy told him.

'Where'd tha get coat hangers?'

'From tree that grows 'em, daft.'

Isaac swung on the gate watching the sky again and I looked up at it too but I wasn't used to the vast sky like Isaac was and it frightened me. Strange that, how in only a matter of a few hundred yards the community's make-up can change. The miner never sees the sky, so there's an inborn fear of it, whereas the farmer works in the sky. So, to the farmer's lad who lies on his back and stares at it all day, the sky presents no threat at all. Young Doctor Cartwright would have said that it was genetic. I looked away from the feathery clouds.

'I know a place,' Isaac told us.

'Where?'

'O'er yon.'

'What sort of place?' I asked.

'It's a hut. An old wood hut, o'er yon.'

'Will tha tek us?'

'Ay. Come on, I'll tek thee.'

Isaac led us over the fields to the river bank. The woody nightshade and the dog-rose were in flower and bent men were sowing turnips silently in another field. Then we passed Simmonds' dye works, where the river smelled of marzipan and where my aunt Henrietta had found all the red fishes floating upside down, and beyond the dye works we came upon Isaac's wooden hut. There were hearts carved all over it. Hearts with arrows through them and with initials carved at each end of the arrow. The boy untied a bit of string on the door and we followed him inside.

'It smells,' I said.

'It smells of women,' Isaac told us.

'Women?' Billy asked whilst poking about in a dark corner. 'Tha means women?' he then said, unable to find another way of describing them.

'Ay, tha naws, rumpin'.'

We looked at him blankly though I had an inkling of what he was getting at. I'd heard about farmers' boys. They watched cows and lambs being born. They knew a thing or two, did farmers' boys.

'Tha means rumpin',' I said, also bereft of synonym.

'Ay. It smells of cunt.'

Billy and I looked at one another again. We were unsure whether we wished to keep our coat hangers anywhere near to women, irrespective of how they smelled.

'Well, tha'd better get tha coat hangers and bring 'em afore someone pinches 'em,' Isaac said, hurrying our decision. 'Shall I help thee to carry 'em?'

'Ay.' We ran off to Aken Jugs and uncovered the stash of coat hangers. Then we carried them as quickly as we could to the hut and laid them in a sloppy pile in the corner where Billy had been searching about.

'What's tha want them for?' Isaac asked.

'Respectability,' I told the clapper boy and Billy looked at me hard wondering if that was the reason he wanted them too. I swore the other two to absolute secrecy and took one of the hangers from its pile and stuffed it in my trousers.

'They'll see that,' Billy said, referring to the beady-eyed members of my family. 'They'll see that, then what use is us secret?'

'What's tha want it for, anyroad?' Isaac asked.

'It's for Mr Brown,' I answered. 'We can trust 'im. I need it to try summat out.'

'What summat?'

'I can't tell thee, not yet.'

The other two looked at one another, wondering how far they might trust me.

'Alreet,' Isaac said, 'tek off tha shirt.' I removed my coarse wool jersey revealing my pale skinny body to the two boys in the gloom of the wooden hut. Isaac took the shirt from me and put the hanger inside like he was going to hang it up in a posh shop. 'Reet, put it on again,' he instructed.

I put my head through the hole and pulled myself into the uncomfortable contraption which Isaac had just prepared. He walked around me once or twice then he said, 'Alreet, tha can go home like that. Nobody'll notice owt.' I walked home with Billy, unable to put my arms straight at my sides and with a wire hook digging uncomfortably into the back of my head. My mother wanted to know why I appeard to walk in such a peculiar manner. I told her that I had become muscle-bound with swinging on too many branches at Aken Jugs.

The following day when nobody else was about I gave the coat hanger to Mr Brown.

'It's for tha Sunday suit,' I said.

'By, it's grand,' he commented. 'Very posh, the Savoy, eh? That's real posh.'

'I found it for thee, Mr Brown. It's for tha Sunday suit.'

'Well, I thank thee, lad. Thank thee,' he said and I stared into his sky blue eyes begging him.

'Tha wants summat?' he asked.

I nodded.

'Oh, ay,' he said and produced a bag from his waistcoat pocket and wheezed into it. He exploded it at me but he could see by my face that it wasn't yet another demonstration of his *Wonderful, wonderful* that I needed. The lodger then stood up, put his hand into his trouser pocket and rattled the loose change which lay in a heavy lump on his thigh. He gave me a threepenny piece.

'Is it worth thruppence?' I asked excitedly.

'Ay, lad, all of that.'

I showed him the shiny silver coin. 'How many of tha paper bags will this buy?' I asked him.

'Thirty-six.'

'Reet, Mr Brown. I'll have thirty-six of tha paper bags then,' and I pressed the money back into the lodger's hand.

'Well, I can't right now,' he said, 'but I'll get 'em for thee, lad, don't tha worry, I'll have 'em for thee. Now thee put tha money aways and don't spend owt, mind, and I'll get the bags from my factory. Will that be satisfactory?' He smiled at me, his prospective buyer, with his blue eyes and I nodded excitedly as my grandmother came through the door dressed in her outdoor coat and with an enormous parcel in her outstretched hands. She seemed to have it balanced at the back edge with the tip of her nose though the heavy parcel rose way above her head. She slammed it down on to the dining table, like a seal ridding itself of a tiresome object.

'What's tha got there, Grandmother?'

'It's a parcel, lad. From th'aunt Henrietta Tsiblitz.'

'Well, what's in it?' I asked, noting the large amount of Mr Brown's paper that it had taken to wrap it.

'I don't know, puddin', tha'll 'ave to wait till it's open.' She tugged at the layers of paper.

'I'll bet tha med a lotta money from the Germans when tha sold 'em that,' I told our lodger. He smiled at my grandmother as she continued to unwrap the parcel.

'What's tha bin tellin' him now?' she asked but the lodger only continued to smile.

Lancaster came into the room and, sniffing the air, said, 'Rubber. I know that smell, Mother, it's them suits that Mr Tsiblitz used to bring with him.'

Sure enough, my grandmother had unwrapped a neatly

folded pile of rubber clothing and was now reading an accompanying letter from the sender which she had found at the bottom of the parcel.

'Ay, it's them smelly rubber suits. I remember the feel of that stuff,' Lancaster told us as he let his fingers ripple through the cold and folded garments while his mother's eyes scanned what had been written in the correspondence.

'Not exactly,' said Emily.

'No?' asked Mr Brown, eager for an explanation.

'No. It's Mr Tsiblitz's latest invention to help fight fires.'

Lancaster had by now removed several articles of rubber from the neat pile and was looking critically at them. 'Can't see how this will fight a fire, Mother,' he said.

His mother slapped his hand and told him to stop playing about with the clothing then she read aloud from the letter. 'They are fire-fighting suits,' she explained, 'and they come in three parts. There's a cape . . . ' Here Lancaster, disobeying his mother, grabbed the rubber cape and put it about his shoulders. It was very long like a policeman's cape and it almost touched the floor. 'Then there is the helmet,' my grandmother continued. My uncle slipped the helmet over his head but in truth it was more of a hood than a helmet. It too was made from rubber and it had a visor through which one could see, though the material clearly wasn't made of glass, and there was a peculiar metal disc which had holes all around its edge and which lay flat on the top of my uncle's head; the hood was long and met the cape at the shoulders, completely hiding his clothes. A piece of rubber hose trailed from the back of the hood. The third and final part of the uniform was a pair of rubber trousers which Lancaster pulled over his ordinary clothes and snapped to his waist beneath the cape with strong elastic. They were much too long for him and for a minute or two he stomped about our parlour like a Martian in flippers. Eventually he sat down on one of the dining chairs

59

and he removed the hood to reveal his red and sweating face.

'By, it's hot in here,' he said, blowing out his cheeks, 'and that helmet thing weighs a ton.'

'What's that tube for?' I asked, pointing to the length of hose which hung at the back of the hood and which my uncle now held in his hands.

'Dunno,' he said.

'Watter,' said our lodger. The engineer in Mr Brown was now coming out.

'Watter?' I asked.

'Ay. Watter. It's fire-fighting equipment, isn't it? What else will tha fight the fire with if it's not watter?'

'Tha'll get some strange things from my Lancaster's head, Mr Brown, but tha'll not get watter from it,' my grandmother said defensively.

'No, look at it t'other end, Mrs Brightside. Tha fixes loose end of hose to watter tap.'

'And fills my Lancaster's head with watter?' My grandmother was quite indignant at the thought of it, but Mr Brown was a patient man.

'Ay, in a manner of speaking. Look, watter will come out of this 'ere disc, them's 'oles in it, sithee,' he said, pointing to the disc which had been laid flat on my uncle's head and which presumably was responsible for the helmet weighing the ton.

'And then what?'

'Then tha can put out fire. The disc will spin round, throwing out the watter and putting out the fire.'

'Well, why not just have a length of tube? Why tek watter through the fireman's head?' my grandmother asked with exasperation.

'So he can rescue them who's caught up in flames, Mrs Brightside. If I see it correctly, the fireman can wander into the heat of the conflagration with his own watter all about and keeping down the flames, and at the same time have his hands free to make his rescue and keep the poor soul free from further burns, too, while the watter whizzes o'er him.'

'Brilliant,' said Lancaster.

'Mr Brown, tha's a genius,' I said.

'Ay, well, I suppose it's Mr Tsiblitz who'll be the genius,' Mr Brown said uncomfortably. 'He invented it.'

'How many suits are there, Mother?' Lancaster asked.

'There's six, one for each of the members of the fire-fighting team. Your aunt says that she was sorry to learn of the fire at the Gills' house and Mr Tsiblitz thought that a present of half a dozen suits would prevent anything like that from happening again. Buckets is past, she says, we must progress with the world, tha naws.' Then she said, 'Tha'd better go and get Wenceslas Piggott, it's him who'll be wanting them.'

Lancaster went off to get the schoolteacher and brought him to our house a few minutes later. My grandmother showed Wenceslas Piggott the suits and Mr Brown explained how he thought they might work.

'Ay, that's all very well, Mr Brown,' he said, 'but where does tha find six watter taps, eh?'

'I can see tha's not an educator for nothin',' Mr Brown told him. 'Tha leave that with me, lad. I'm no schoolteacher but I've bin a fine engineer in my time and I should think I could rig up summat for thee. Tha naws, a single hose feeding all six fire fighters, sithee.'

During the following week Mr Brown turned out a modification to the original design and built the suits into a single fire-fighting unit, but he made it so that each suit was detachable and the end product was a fire-fighting unit of anything from one to six men. The main thing was that no matter how many men there were in the team, they were plugged into a single water point. Wenceslas Piggott was so impressed that he invited Mr Brown to join the brigade and our lodger then officially replaced the one-legged Charlie Gill. At first Charlie objected but Mr Piggott, to demonstrate the futility of Charlie's membership, made him put

61

on one of the suits and connected it to the tap in our scullery and every time the disc on his head spun round, flinging out its water, the one-legged Charlie spun round too. Then finally he fell over and every time he tried to stand up the disc, which continued its dizzy spinning, flung him over again. All that water was making the ground very muddy anyway and Charlie couldn't find any purchase on the common. He ended up scrabbling in a sea of mud and he started to cry. Mrs Gill had to come and get him and take him indoors and Wenceslas stood on the common apologising to their closed door again whilst Charlie's mother gave her son a bath in the tin tub in front of their fire.

Seeing Charlie Gill's performance wasn't enough; Billy and I couldn't wait for the brigade to demonstrate the true value of Elyahou Tsiblitz's latest invention, not to mention the genius of Mr Brown's modification. Time passed without fires and we became impatient. One day Mr Brown called me to him and slipped me thirty-six paper bags with a blue-eyed wink. I handed him his silver threepenny piece and asked him how many bags he would exchange for another forty Savoy hangers each as pristine as the one which he had received from me before. One thousand and summat seemed to be so many that I wondered if they might not fill the whole of the wooden hut. Billy and I ran off there to stash away the paper bags and to assess our storage space. As we crossed the fields – jugs and crimbles – we could see the small figure of Isaac standing on an upturned bucket and peering into the hut through a small window. The window was high up near the roof and no bigger than the thickness of a miner's forearm.

'What's up, Isaac?' I called.

'Shh. It's rumpin'. They're rumpin' in there,' he told us.

'Women?' Billy asked in a knowing kind of way.

'Ay. What else?' The clapper boy looked puzzled.

'Tha never naws,' Billy said. 'How many?'

'How many what, Billy?'

'How many women's rumpin' in there, daft?'

'Just one, like allus.'

Billy couldn't see why so much fuss was being created over a single rumpin' woman and I couldn't understand what they were on about anyway. I climbed on to the bucket and peered in through the dirty window expecting to see a rumpin' woman and was surprised to see in the gloom of the hut a man without his trousers. He seemed to be rolling madly about the floor and possessed by demons. My grandfather might have said that he was a man struggling with his soul and I was about to impart this nugget of wisdom to my companions when I put my foot through the rusting base of the bucket and my leg started to bleed.

'It's nowt,' I told the others whilst we all sat on the grass. Interest in the activities in the hut had ceased. I tore a piece from my silk French knickers and tied a bandage round my leg.

'Well, buckets bust,' Isaac told us and he lay on the grass and watched the sky. Billy and I lay on our stomachs, our noses only inches from the ground. We had a genetic propensity to lie in an eighteen-inch seam, that's what Doctor Cartwright was later to tell our mothers. 'We could smoke buggers out, like ratten',' Isaac said to a passing cloud.

'Ay, that'd do it,' Billy said and with a sudden flurry of activity we had collected sufficient wood and twigs to make a small fire in front of the hut. We tried to waft the smoke under the tight-fitting door. From the lack of response within we concluded that the smoke was not getting through. Then with the sudden realisation that here was the ideal opportunity to call the newly equipped fire fighters into operation, I said, 'I'll run and ring t'bell,' and I hared off to the schoolhouse. Mr Brown and Rube Hardwick came from the pub and the three strapping miners dashed up from the pit and congregated in the school yard. Carrying their suits, they followed me across the fields in the direction of the wispy smoke. When we arrived the door was just about scorching and Isaac said to Mr Brown, 'Tha'd better get in quick, there's two people in there,' and I said, 'Never mind people, Mr Brown, us forty Savoy hangers are in there.'

Mr Brown instructed the other four to put on their suits.

'Where's Mr Piggott?' asked one of the miners. 'He should be instructin', not thee.'

'Bugger Mr Piggott,' said Mr Brown. 'Come on, we've important work to do, get tha bloody suits on.' He ran off to Simmonds' dye works with a long length of hose, presumably looking for a water tap. When the brigade had got their suits on Billy went to tell Mr Brown to turn on the tap and Isaac and I could hear the water as it ran, picking up speed in the pipe, but when it finally arrived at our lodger's contraption the water seemed to take the line of least resistance and come only through one of the discs, flinging the unfortunate miner to the ground and dragging the other three bodies on top of him like collapsing cards.

'Turn the bloody thing off,' I heard him shout from under the pile of bodies. 'Tha's connected it to hot watter tap.'

He lay on his back with the disc whizzing round on top of his head but the spray was not falling anywhere near to the flames. The other men were trying to disentangle themselves, but every time they scrambled up, the force of the water away from them kept dragging them back on to the yelling miner. Isaac then showed what a bright lad he was by standing on the main pipe, thus cutting off the water supply and giving all four men the opportunity to get to their feet. He then took his foot from the hose and the water this time found itself in the helmet of the man at the other end. He screamed, tried to escape from the hot water by running away, fell over and dragged the others on top of him. Now it was his turn to lie on his back with his disc spinning dizzily, unable to raise himself from the ground.

The door now appeared to be fully alight but there were no screams from within the hut, just a few grunts like Mr Doyle's pigs might make. Suddenly the flow of water stopped; Mr Brown must have got the message and turned off the tap. Then with all four men standing upright the water was switched on again and now it was cold water that whizzed and swirled from the discs on the top of each man's head. This was what we had wanted to see – the new German fire-fighting force – and how magnificent they were, too, as in no time at all they put out the fire. Rube Hardwick was battering at the smoking door with his shoulder when his disc stopped its spinning altogether and his share of the water for some reason channelled internally rather than through the equipment on the top of his head. A steady stream of cold water flowed from the bottom of his rubber trousers. The discs belonging to the two men on either side of him were working perfectly, though, and the circling tensions of the waters seemed to ripple a strange torsion into the innkeeper and his rubber equipment, lifting him some nine or ten inches from the ground between his two larger companions. The water continued to trickle from his trousers: from behind he appeared to be taking a leak whilst suspended in mid-air. In this hovering, almost angel-like posture, Rube managed to rip the door from its hinges and flung it, still smouldering, to the ground. As Mr Brown dashed back up from the dye-works he saw his team disappear through the dark doorway to reappear moments later. One man carried the naked Wenceslas Piggott over his shoulder. His moustache drooped in a bedraggled silence and water whizzed about his befuddled brain. A second man had grabbed up the curved and white nakedness of Marlene Jellis, whose beautiful red hair managed to cover all those bits in which we boys at last showed mild interest and which might have given Billy and me insight into how the unfinished portrait at the back of the classroom in Standard One might one day appear.

Fortunately the hangers were safe. Billy and I stashed our bags in a dry corner and the following day Isaac brought his father to the damaged hut. He was a man much older than I thought he would be, perhaps as old as my grandfather. He carried a shotgun over his shoulder like an old soldier and he leaned it against the side of the hut whilst he set about rehanging the scorched door.

Mr Brown improved his original design of the fire-fighting equipment by incorporating valves in the six individual hoses. Each man was then able to control the flow to his own disc, thereby putting rationality as well as water into the system. We had a few fires after that but none ended in the chaos that Mr Brown had promoted that day.

5

The flower opens to take in the news

Prior to my being ten years old, Jacky Jellis brought the news. Apart from the Bellman we didn't have a lot of visitors to the village. There were one or two travelling salesmen, that's all. In the old days, long before I was born, there had of course been Elyahou Tsiblitz. Then there was the tailor with the tape measure round his neck who sold us our suits on the drip, then the man who sold us our spectacles from his tray of lenses; though he was long-sighted and she was short-sighted, my grandparents shared their glasses and couldn't imagine that there would be anything wrong in the practice. After all, they were married, she told those who bothered to enquire. There had even been a man who brought around window frames which he carried on his back as if it was about to break and there was the midden man who shovelled the shit from the ash heaps and carted it away in his wagon, but none of these people brought us news. Only Jacky Jellis brought the news. Then when I was ten years old, that will have been in 1923, three things happened, all of which opened up the trumpet of the flower which Jacky said that our village was – suddenly, very suddenly the village didn't seem to be as remote and as cut off from civilisation as it had been.

Firstly, in the spring some men came and planted a signpost at the crossroads beyond the big house. The signpost had three white arms, all at right angles to each other; they pointed in the directions of Leeds, Castleford and Wakefield and were intended to be for the assistance of the motorists. Needless to say, the fourth road, the one which led down to our village and to nowhere else except to

Hunger Hill, didn't warrant a positional arm on the post. On a spring day from the village you could distantly hear the traffic at the crossroads, the honking of horns and the rub of tyres on the rutted road. It was all mixed in with the calls of the willow wren and the chiff-chaff and the buzzing of the insects and the cycling of the wheel at the pit head, but you couldn't see it. Nothing came down our way.

During that spring the ground ivy grew up the post, almost obliterating the signs, and a family of thrushes built their nest right at the top of the pole. It wore the nest like a hat and we lads had to be careful when cutting back the green tangle of leaves so that the goggled motorists wouldn't have any difficulty in finding their ways. Then one day as Billy and I sat in the dust watching the Hillmans, the Calcotts and the Model T Fords chugging by or turning at the intersection, we had a brainwave. We turned the post through an angle of ninety degrees and directed all the Leeds-bound traffic down to our village. Consequently we had a steady stream of traffic tootling past the terrace, digging up the common and coming to an abrupt stop where the track petered out at the foot of Hunger Hill. The traffic would then have to swing round in an arc and head back the way it had come. Sometimes a motorist would ask, 'Can I get to Leeds up here?' and point up the dangerous slope of Hunger Hill and Billy would say, 'Ay. Just keep goin',' and invite the poor man to take his motor on the precipitous journey.

When it rained the ground would become extremely boggy at that end of the village and the motors would get themselves embedded in the mud. Billy and I – and sometimes Isaac if he could get away from Owler Crimble – would, for a penny each, offer to help get the car out from where it had stuck. We once got a posh yellow Napier stuck half-way up Hunger Hill and nobody could budge it, not even the colliers could budge it, so the motorist left it there rusting on the hill, until all its bits had been stolen by other motorists who broke it up piece by piece. Eventually everything went, except the four wheels, that is, which remained firmly embedded in the mud and are there to this day. One day a motorist, having climbed Hunger Hill and given Billy and me twopence each to help him carry down one of the doors from the Napier, spied the Jam Sahib's motor car parked outside our house. He was just about to rip off one of the lights at the front of the motor when my father came from the house and beat the man to the ground – he drove away with the yellow door but I don't think that he ever came back.

The new influx of traffic brought more strangers into our village in a single day than it had received in a hundred years. And these were people only too eager to speak, to tell not internalised salesmen's stories like yarns told by characters in a book – no, like the Bellman, they wanted to tell you things, real things about the outside world.

Did tha naw that the Duke of York had married Lady Elizabeth Bowes Lyon? Did tha naw that there was a Cup Final at London? Wembley? Did tha naw that Bolton Wanderers had won the Cup, my team tha naws? Fancy, Billy and I had met a man from Bolton Wanderers. He might as well have been from the other side of the planet, so strange and wonderful was he. Did tha naw that Mr Baldwin had become the Prime Minister? Did tha naw that we'd signed a peace treaty with Turkey? I didn't naw that we was at war with Turkey, I told Billy. Did tha naw that Mount Etna had erupted? Did tha naw that there had been an earthquake in Japan? There were a million questions, a million pieces of information all from the men who had lost their ways in the motors. Now, here was education. Cubitt, Buick, Calthorpe, Lagonda, Riley, Vulcan, Austin, Clyno, Humber, Jowett. Now, here was education, being driven at breakneck speed down the hill and into our village.

It was a glorious summer's day when they brought the electricity. It slipped silently in the soft mosses at the summit of Hunger Hill. It crept noiselessly among the flowers. It got in the yellow rattle and the common veronica, it stepped quietly over rock rose and gromwell and the great stitchwort. It got entangled in the bindweed and the woodbine and among the red poppies. The cherries were ripe and it shook them from the trees. Nothing could stop it and it came right into the house. Nobody knew what to make of it, not really. Ernest said that you could see the water and taste it, it wasn't like water. Nor was it like the gas. Although the gas had never actually been taken into the house, you knew the gas at the lamp standard. You could smell the gas – like when Clarrie and I had whooping cough we could certainly smell the gas. But the electricity didn't have a smell and it came in wires and it brought us something which we knew very well. It brought us light. That's how it was, completely alien yet bringing us something as commonplace as light. It was difficult to make much of that. Yet it was fitting that I should have thought it to be travelling in the flowers. All those Latin names which nobody understood; but it was those same flowers described by such lack of understanding which gave us the commonplace too. They gave us the colours – red and rose and yellow and blue. Sometimes at night it was silent no more, probably because the flowers had gone to sleep, and it hummed in its wires and I would lie awake listening to the owls and the electricity and the severed voices. When it rained, it hummed all the more and the metal in the rain turned to acid and that was a new taste for us to experience. It was then that I knew that this stuff was different. It had a power. It could kill you. It came from a long way off and it came right into our house.

One day in the autumn, Mr Brown arrived home with a large cardboard box full of bits of wire and wood and string and raspberries. He gave the fruit to my mother, telling her that he had found them on the bushes down by Bottom Boat as he walked back from Kippax.

70

'Why did you go to Kippax, Mr Brown?' she asked him.

'To get this lot, love,' he told her and waved his hand like a magician over the boxful of wonderful things.

'What is it?'

'It's stuff to make a crystal set.'

'What's a crystal set?' I asked.

'A wireless, lad, a wireless,' he said excitedly.

I watched Mr Brown constructing his wireless. He made a wooden base for it. Then he wound some copper wire on to a cardboard tube and he called this the inductance. He mounted it on to the wooden base with some brass screws and fitted some slider bars on to it. He then showed me a bornite crystal and told me that he was going to bring voices out of the other side of Hunger Hill and make the voices speak through his crystal. I asked if it would be like the voices I could hear caught up in the winding wheel or like those I heard at night whilst lying in bed with my mother and he told me that they would be just the same. He set the crystal into a brass cup, using some molten metal to hold it there, and when it was ready he set that into the wooden base too. This he called the detector. Then he fixed down a thing which he called a condenser. He took a length of wire through our window and attached one end to a screw on the inductance and walked with the other end all the way to the gas lamp on the common. He shinned up the pole like a monkey and tied the wire to the very top, then he slid down and came back to the house. He told me that this was an aerial. He then took a second length of wire and attached it to another screw on the inductance. He tied the other end of this wire to the cold tap in our scullery sink. He called this length of wire the earth. Then he asked me to place a pair of headphones over my ears and he moved the sliders on the inductance. I heard a high pitched squeak which then disappeared as he continued to move the slider, then the set blew up in our faces as we sat there looking at it. After the initial bang I sadly watched one of the wires burning

71

weakly then give out, and Mr Brown said, 'Bugger it. I'll have to insert a switch.'

He then put a switch into the circuit, fixed up the burned wires and asked me to put on the headphones again. For a second or two I could hear people talking then the voices went. I hadn't heard what had been said. Mr Brown looked with a screwed-up eye at the ticking clock which sat at the centre of our mantelshelf. Then he looked at me thoughtfully. 'It's nearly six o'clock,' he told me with a nod and with his eye still screwed. 'Go get Rosanne. She should hear this. I'm going to get the time signal from Paris. Go on, lad, go and get her.'

I went over to the wagon and asked Rosanne to come and see Mr Brown's new invention and she came back to the house with me and put on the headphones. At six o'clock precisely Mr Brown put the slider to a wavelength of 2600 metres and Rosanne heard some pips. They weren't English pips, they were French pips and Mr Brown was satisfied for he had thought that it was only right that a French person should be the first to hear a broadcast from France in our house. Rosanne danced from the house as happy as if her own father had been talking to her from Paris. The fact that she had only heard a time signal made not the slightest difference, France had spoken with one of her daughters not just across Hunger Hill but across hundreds and hundreds of miles. And she'd spoken in our house.

After that a whole web of wires spread from the houses in our terrace. They came out of windows and were fixed to the gas lamp on the common. The aerial wires gradually became more sophisticated than that which Mr Brown had strung up. Some were slung from chimney pot to pole and these Rosanne used to walk over, practising her high wire tricks and teaching Clarrie to do the same. They were both dressed in sequinned tights and had ostrich feathers in their hair. I was ten years old, Clarrie was eight, and I realised at last that she was no longer a pot dog. I think that I was in love with her.

Gradually, as more crystal sets grew in our houses and as outside the web of wiring became more complex, we heard less and less from the broadcasters and more and more of what was going on in each other's homes. For a time, eavesdropping become a popular pastime, all information being relayed via the gas lamp on the common. Then one day Mr Archbold bought a commercial wireless set with knobs and dials and a plug to go in an electric socket. We could see through his window and watched him and his whole family bathed in a yellow light, sitting there in their parlour and listening to the world together. Gradually we all got them and tuned into the world. The aerials stayed up though and Rosanne and Clarrie were often seen dancing at night on the web of wires beneath the diamond cold stars.

6

'Say nowt 'bout us poverty, it's a bloody secret'

The immediate post-war mood of confidence and militancy among the miners didn't last long. Fear for the future once again took a hold as trade became depressed and the labour market declined with it. The government had taken control of the mines during the War but in 1921 Lloyd George gave control back to the owners. That happened to coincide with falling markets, falling prices and reduced profits. At the same time as asking his men to take a cut in wages, my maternal grandfather, like all other coal owners, took the opportunity of ridding his pits of the most troublesome men. The hotheads were booted out – and good riddance, said Jacky Jellis who thought he knew what was going on.

There was no peace of mind in our household despite the familial ties; Ernest was bent up with his arthritis and Mr Brown was beginning to spit up great black gobbets of muck, just like Sidall Junkin had once done. Neither of them could count on a secure wage, even a reduced one. Young Doctor Cartwright told them both that it would be only a matter of time before they would be forced to pack in their work. But Ernest said that he wasn't about to retire and that he would be hewing the coal until he dropped; then Mr Brown told him that the doctor hadn't quite meant it in the way in which it was put. No. What the doctor meant was that he and Ernest, because of their poor health, would be the next to be made to leave the pit. If they were lucky they might be given light jobs grading the coal at the surface but their wages would be halved if they did that.

'Well, I'll not do it,' Ernest told him. 'They'll not 'ave me sorting coal till it's time.'

'Oh, ay, they will,' said Mr Brown. 'And I'll tell thee why, Ernest. It's because tha's got no political clout, lad, that's why.'

'No clout!' exclaimed my shocked grandfather. 'What's tha think the union is? It's a funny sort of no clout is that.'

'No, Ernest, tha's not hearing me. I said no *political* clout. Oh, ay, the union can mek a noise, it can mek a noise as far as Barnsley and I grant thee that's a long road. But the capitalists can mek a commotion a lot further than that, lad. They can mek a row all o'er bloody country and that's political clout, that is.' My grandfather looked glum. 'The only hope is to support the Labour Party and try to organise us selves into a political force – that's what we must hope for Ernest, sithee.'

Mr Brown was right. The Labour Party was just that – a band of hope. That was the weakness of the Labour Party; it was no more than a rag-bag of supporting voices of working people and most of them were saying, 'I want to work' and 'I want a decent living wage' and 'I want decent working conditions.' But there was no ideology because those same voices had no time for ideology. They were just stranded voices like those I heard every night when I lay there in my mother's bed.

I want a job.

My family needs a living wage.

I need to cough this shit out of my lungs.

When Ramsay MacDonald in 1921 was moved to tell that the weakness of the party was the 'fault of the minds of the people' that's what he meant. They had no ideology, they had no theory, they knew where they wanted to be but they hadn't a clue how they should get there. Billy and me though – we knew how to get there. It needed inspiration like the turning of the signpost. And so did Mr Brown – he knew how to get there, that was his genius.

Early in 1924 there was a lock-out at the pit. Trouble had been rumbling on for years, ever since Thwaite had taken back control. There had been a lock-out in 1921 culminating

75

in the miners' capitulation on Black Friday. There had been lock-outs in each subsequent year, a week here and a week there. The miners never won anything. The coal price fell and so did wages. Then in 1924 Thwaite asked the men to accept another cut. He wandered on the common in his silk top hat and frock coat, walking amongst the young lads and a few dogs who played cricket with a real cork ball. Then he sat like a king in the rubber chair holding his cane like a sceptre and he shouted to the assembled pitmen, 'If tha won't see sense and tek a cut in wages then I'll close up pit,' and he got up and walked back to the big house jeered all the way by the colliers.

After a few days we knew that the lock-out was going to last and our house was running out of money. My grandfather called a meeting of the family and all who lived at the house. There was Grandmother and Grandfather and William and my mother; Lancaster and Albert were there and so were Rosanne and Mr Brown. They all sat around the dining table in the parlour and tried to work out a strategy for survival whilst Clarrie and I sat on the pegged rug in front of the fire. My grandmother who was a proud, proud woman said that she wasn't about to fall back on the parish and told us that anyone who wanted to live on charity had better leave right away. She wasn't going to ask the local shopkeepers for extended credit either; tick was for those without self-respect, she said, cutting down our options at a stroke.

'But if tha rules out charity and tha rules out local credit, Mother, what's left?' Albert asked.

'Sell up,' said Lancaster glumly. He still worried about following Archie Jellis down to London and agreement to sell up would have eased his own difficult paths to decision.

'There's nowt to sell, lad,' my grandfather said, poking a matchstick in his ears and scraping the wax on to the side of his matchbox.

'That's typical, isn't it, all tha's got is a box of Vestas and a bit of wax and tha tells us to say nowt 'bout us poverty as if it's all a bloody secret.' My father scorned his parents.

'Now, William, careful 'ow tha speaks to tha mother,' Ernest warned and my father sat back angrily in his chair.

'Pawnbroker.' Mr Brown spoke suddenly and emphatically and they all turned to look at him. 'Will tha stand for t'pawnbroker, Mrs Brightside?' he asked my grandmother. She was unsure if falling back on the pawnbroker demonstrated a loss of self-respect or not and was unable to answer the lodger. 'I go to pawnbroker regular,' he confided to his stunned audience. 'Nowt wrong in that. I pawn my Sunday suit on a Monday if I'm stuck for a few bob and I reclaims it of a Saturday when I gets my wage. Now tell me, what if anything is wrong in that?'

'Like my husband says, we've nowt to sell,' my grandmother told him coldly. 'If we've nowt to sell then we've nowt to pawn.' She sat with her hands hidden in her pinafore pocket and stared poker-faced at the lodger. 'And I'll not pawn the furniture,' she told him. 'Now that is a lack of self-respect, Mr Brown, pawning the furniture brings nowt but shame.'

'What about tha Sunday best?' Mr Brown asked.

'I'll not have us going off to church in rags,' she said and my grandfather nodded in agreement. 'I'd have thought tha would understand that, Mr Brown.'

'Oh, I do, I do,' he concurred.

'The Brightside family has a respect in this community, Mr Brown,' she went on, 'and it'll stay that way. We may be destitute but by God we'll not show it,' she told the lodger, and my grandfather murmured his approval of her bold statement whilst my father squirmed in his chair. There was a long silence which was only broken by Mr Brown's voice once again.

'Tell me, Mrs Brightside, if tha'd got two Sunday best, if each of the members of tha family had two sets of Sunday best, would that give thee more or less respect?'

'Why, more of course,' she answered.

'And if tha'd got two sets each would tha have any objection to the pawning of one of them sets?'

'None, Mr Brown. Of course I wouldn't. But we don't have two sets of best, do we? We have only the one.'

The lodger turned to Albert and all were attentive of what he was about to say. 'Tha naws that chap who comes o'er from Leeds, the tailor with the tape around 'is neck?'

'Ay.'

'Well, 'e'll mek up clothes on drip, won't 'e?'

'Ay.'

My grandmother put on the shared glasses, hoping, I think, that she might be able to hear better the gem of an idea that was about to fall from Mr Brown's lips. However, she couldn't see anything through them at such short distance and took them off, turning her ear to him instead.

'Now suppose we instruct him to mek a set of best for each of us. Mek 'em quick and payment on the drip. Then we teks 'em straight o'er to the pawnshop, how's that sound?'

'Brilliant,' said Albert.

'Ay, it's an idea,' said Ernest, though looking cautiously for my grandmother's reaction. 'What's tha think, luv?'

My grandmother was silent, mulling over Mr Brown's suggestion. 'Well, I can't see owt wrong in that,' she said at last. 'Not yet, anyroad.'

'It'll bring in some money. Quite a bit of money, Mrs Brightside,' the lodger encouraged her.

'Ay, but will it be enough to see us through this 'ere lock-out?' Ernest asked.

'Well, it won't last more than a month, will it?'

'Probably not, but will it bring in enough to see us through the month?'

'I should think so,' said the lodger. 'Sithee, there's summat I've not told thee.'

'What's that, Mr Brown?' my grandmother asked suspiciously.

'Well, it happened a bit since did this, but tha Donald is

sittin' on the key to a fortune.' My ears pricked up at the mention of my name. 'The little lad comes to me and 'e brings with 'im a clothes hanger. A fancy clothes hanger from the Savoy Hotel in London.' I felt the discomfort at the back of my neck as all eyes fell upon me. 'Now, don't go on at lad,' said the lodger, 'e did the right thing, did the little lad. Like I say, 'e brung me this 'ere coat hanger and I hung my Sunday best on it. That's what the lad said it was for anyroad. Am I right, Donald?' I nodded. 'Well, when I next took my suit to the pawnshop, it were on this 'ere coat hanger, sithee, and Mr Partridge, instead of giving me five shillings like he normally did, he gives us ten. Ten bob for a Sunday best. Well, at first I thought there must be some mistake but I says nowt, like. Then next time I takes my suit in to him, I gets ten bob again. So I says nowt again like and I thinks, well, must be, but just to test I take it the next time without the hanger and guess what?'

'Tha gets five bob for it,' Ernest said.

'That's right, Ernest, five bob. So I sticks it back on the coat hanger and I tek it down to Mr Zermansky over in Leeds after that and guess what?'

'Tha gets ten bob again,' Ernest said.

'No. I don't Ernest. I don't get ten bob at all. Mr Zermansky gives us fifteen.'

'Fifteen shillings?' my grandmother said disbelievingly.

'Ay.'

'For a Sunday best?'

'Ay. I tell thee them coat hangers is worth a fortune and tha little lad 'as gotten forty of the buggers.' He winked at my father. 'So what I have to suggest is this. We get tailor in to mek us suits and dresses. Even the two young uns. That'll be ten lots of clothes and we put 'em all on the lad's hangers, then we teks 'em round to different pawnshops – spread it about a bit like, so none of 'em get to askin' questions. We puts us other Sunday best on when we do it, like, then we'll look posh and the Savoy hangers won't appear to be out of place. Tha naws, we can put on a bit of a show, posh up the accents, that kind of thing. Then we let the word out a bit, tell one or two of the neighbours, them with a bit of brass tucked away like Mr Doyle, and we offer to sell 'em one of the surplus hangers, say for two and sixpence – that way they'll be able to get an extra five bob from the pawnbroker if they come to pawn owt. It'll be an investment for a man like Doyle. What's tha say?'

'Mr Brown, tha's a genius,' I told him from my perch on the rug.

The others remained non-committal, looking from one to the other.

'We'll still 'ave us self-respect,' Ernest told my grandmother.

'And going out of a weekday in us Sunday best will be a right treat for the neighbours,' my father then told her.

'Not to mention pawning tha Sunday best whilst all got up in a second best,' reminded Mr Brown. 'That's real posh, that is.'

'But what of the expense of the new clothes?' my grand-mother asked.

'It's on drip,' Mr Brown said.

'Ay, but it'll still cost in time.'

'We're still paying for the last lot, luv,' Ernest said, 'and we had them afore the War. Spread o'er time we'll not notice it.'

Listening to that conversation in our parlour taught me a lot about pride and about respectability and about the self-esteem of our class. But it also taught me about fear. The fear of the dispossessed. There was no way that my grand-mother would have pawned the furniture because, exactly as she had explained to Ernest about Mr Brown's suit, it would have left her family naked and she wasn't having that. Possession and fear were intertwined in a working class community and the fear of nakedness was the worst fear of all. A naked house was just as fearful as a naked body. That's why we had the pot spaniel on the mantelshelf and the two flying ducks on the wall – it dispelled our fears and what is more because they were on display it showed our neighbours that they had been dispelled. In effect it gave us our self-esteem. Lack of fear and our self-esteem were the same thing and it was conferred on us by our neighbours. It was probably for the same reason that Mr Brown had his paper bags; because apart from what he stood in of a Sunday plus a spare brass collar stud, he had nothing. But my knowing of the paper bags, that gave him his self-esteem. And that was probably why I longed to acquire paper bags for myself and why I prized those coat hangers. But *they* had turned out to be something quite different, hadn't they? They were investment. Fancy that. Forty of the buggers at two and six a piece. Like the man said, I was sitting on a fortune and I didn't care that nobody would see them stashed away in a mucky hut. It was like having pound notes in a bank, you put them away and you didn't tell, but you knew where they were and you could afford to smile.

'Well, where's tha coat hangers, lad?' my father said.

I looked at Mr Brown, pleading telepathically, and eventually a liveliness found its way into his blue eyes and he said, 'Don't tha worry 'bout that, William. I've got 'em stashed.' Mr Brown was like lightning.

The following day it rained and Mr Brown came trampling over the wet grass at Owler Crimble and approached Billy, Isaac and me at the hut.

'Expect tha wants paper bags then?' he said, standing at the door with the rain drizzling down on him.

'Don't think much of paper bags. Can't do owt with 'em,' Isaac told him, whirling his clapper at knee height. Mr Brown did a little skip in his baggy trousers like he would have done to avoid a whizzing cricket ball smashing into his shins.

'Can't 'urt thee, daft,' Billy told him.

'What, lad? What's that?'

'Clapper can't 'urt thee, Mr Brown.'

'No, lad, no.' Then after a while he said, 'What's tha want for 'em then?'

The rain was bouncing off his head and small rivulets were running over his nose and down his cheeks and dripping from his chin.

'Tha'd better come in,' I offered and the man came into the hut and sat on some dry potato sacks which Isaac's father had given us for our den.

'We want to sell 'em to thee,' I told him.

'Sell!' exclaimed Mr Brown. Then, rubbing his palm on the wet stubble on his chin, he said, 'Well, I don't know about that. I hadn't expected we should 'ave to buy 'em. Tha naws how tight money is at the moment.' Then he began to cough and he caught one of the great gobbets of muck in his mouth, went to the doorway and spat the black gob as far from the hut as he could manage. Then he came back and sat on the sacks, shaking his head. 'Sell, eh! I'd not considered having to buy 'em,' he said again.

'Well, tha can owe us money, Mr Brown,' Isaac said, looking at the stack of hangers in the corner of the hut, where they had been since that day we had brought them from Aken Jugs.

'Ay, that's a possibility,' the lodger acknowledged more brightly.

'Not for too long, mind,' Billy said.

'Well, 'ow much then?' Mr Brown asked. 'What about sixpence each, that'd be generous?'

'Nivver.' Isaac laughed, scorning the ludicrous offer.

'Two and sixpence,' I said.

'Three shillings,' Isaac topped me quick. 'Three bob or nowt.'

Mr Brown looked stunned. The rain still ran slowly from his hair. 'That's a lot of money, lads. Where shall I find three bob a hanger from?'

'From the pawnshop,' I told him. 'Tha said that Zermansky would give thee ten bob a hanger. Even Partridge gave thee five, tha said so thasen.'

'Ay, but it's not hangers we're pawnin', lad, is it? It's suits we're pawnin'. Hangers are just a way of gettin' more for a suit like I explained to tha grandmother yesterday.'

'Same difference,' Isaac interrupted. For a lad without schooling he was sharp as a tack and from the look in Mr Brown's eye, the lodger knew it.

'Tha's reet, lad,' he said and coughed a little. 'Look tha three, I'll tell thee what'll do. We need one another, us lot, I'm no use without the hangers and tha's got hangers. But tha hangers no good without clothes to hang on 'em, and I'll have the clothes, reet?'

'Reet.'

'So I'll tek ten hangers now and I'll owe thee fifteen bob. One and sixpence per hanger for thee and I get the other one and sixpence for my trouble.'

'Trouble? What trouble would that be, Mr Brown?' Billy asked.

'Negotiation trouble, lad. I'll be the one put out with the pawning of the bloody suits, tha naws. That's trouble.' And he slipped us an enormous blue wink from under his wet forehead.

We nodded our agreement to the deal, each of us appreciative of the trouble to which we were putting the man. Then the four of us spat on our palms and shook hands all round, concluding the transaction.

Mr Doyle had a washable condom which he hung out on the line every morning and, he had to admit, he was ever surprised to find it still there at night when he needed it. Why he imagined that anybody should want to steal his condom was a complete mystery. His new wife, the lass from the next village, was pretty enough but there had always been a suspicion about the pigs. People stayed away from Mr Doyle's condom waving on the line in his small garden at the back of the terrace. It was the last of the condoms brought to our village by Elyahou Tsiblitz. It was a complete rogue – it hadn't developed holes like all the others had. Mr Doyle didn't have unexpected children, he just had pigs. And chickens. Mr Doyle kept chickens as well as pigs, he kept them in a run in the garden too and they were the fattest chickens in Yorkshire. It was fairly common knowledge among the colliers that the reason why his chickens were so fat and healthy was because Mr Doyle fed them with the contents of his condom after it had been used.

Now for sure, one person who did not share this gem of information worthy of a note in the manual of animal husbandry was my grandmother, Emily Brightside. If she had known anything of it, she would not have eaten his chickens and, come to think of it, if she had harboured a suspicion about the other she would never have eaten his pigs either. Yet, had my grandmother been told of it and had she been able to come to terms with the awfulness of Mr Doyle's habit and of course with the chickens' predilection too, then she really would have appreciated the practice as an exercise in masterly economy. Remember 'Waste not, want not' – presumably her motto would have intellectually extended to the use of semen as a protein source for chickens. I only tell you this because during the four weeks of lock-out Mr Brown and Albert stole chickens from Mr Doyle's run on three separate occasions and they gave them to my grandmother to supplement our meagre table rations. Mr Brown lied that he had been able to exchange them for paper bags at Leeds covered market and my grandmother chose not to disbelieve his explanation.

I don't know if the parson knew of Mr Doyle's practice and, if he did, what he might have made of it, but it was he who on one occasion got most of my share of the chicken. Sitting beneath the table, staring at the black gaiters of the man who had been invited to tea, I could only hope that the extra protein might choke him. When you are starving you don't care much for God and his preachermen. Mr Brown didn't care much for them even when he wasn't starving. They gave him the pip and on that occasion, Mr Brown kept on handing me down scraps of food which he took from the plate of the parson, who was sitting next to him. He stole it from his plate when the minister wasn't looking, which was usually when he was busy trying to hide a belch – something he often did. 'Pardon,' he would say with closed eyes and Mr Brown would pass me down another scrap like he would feed a dog out of the sight of the Lord.

Mr Goldenberger came over from Leeds with the tape around his neck and spent a full afternoon measuring each of us up for our new Sunday best. Mr Goldenberger's father was a rabbi and I could never understand how a Jew was able to make Sunday best for a gentile, but he seemed to manage it without complaint so I thought that it must be all right with his Lord. He ran his tape quickly over our bodies a bit at a time and jotted his numbers down in a grubby blue notebook and did a lot of additions sitting on a chair in the parlour with his head in one of his bony hands. He had a dreamy quality about him, as if he might go off to sleep if we were to leave him alone. He reminded me of my duck and of Isaac and I felt sorry for him. After measuring each person he would stop a while, add up his figures and drink deeply from the mugs of tea with which my grandmother plied him. The tea would sometimes drip into his beard and he would suck it from his moustache with nicotine-stained teeth. After all the additions he would then ask us to choose a cloth from a sample book which he carried in his case, but we had already decided that we wanted the most expensive. Then he would give us a price for the job and then another price because we wanted the clothes to be made in a rush. We had rehearsed what we had to say. Then Mr Brown would haggle and usually get ten per cent knocked off the price. When he went away, walking up the hill past

85

the big house, all alone and with his brown case and long beard, it was with the biggest order that Mr Goldenberger had ever received, even if it was to be paid for on the drip.

When the clothes were delivered after only a few days and we had all been fitted we were amazed and delighted at how grand everyone looked. It was a credit to Mr Goldenberger's ability to measure his bits and of course to those whom he employed to follow his instructions. The clothes had been snipped to near perfection and we told the tailor so. He went off again, hundreds of shining pins stuck into his lapels and sucking my grandmother's tea from his moustache. I watched him winding up towards the crossroads and then I watched my duck sleeping on the still skin of water in his rain barrel. Life's diverse philosophies were coming together in my young brain.

My grandfather said that because he was such a clever devil, Mr Brown could do the pawning alone, which of course was a development which the lodger was fully expecting. I guess that he earned his one and sixpence per hanger. He got his usual ten shillings from Mr Partridge at Partridge, Peardorp and Treene in Castleford and he got the fifteen bob from Mr Zermansky. He was dressed in his Sunday best and carried his brass-topped cane like a gentleman. In each shop he visited he passed some comment about not having much time for God, because all that stuff gave him the pip. It seems that it was the only thing he could say in a posh accent but it didn't do his cause much harm because he managed to raise between ten and fifteen shillings in each establishment, and at one in Wakefield – unfortunately it was the last place that he had to go for he would have tried it a second time – he got seventeen and sixpence for Clarrie's dress.

Mr Brown was a real gentleman, there was no messing about. He came straight out to the hut after he had given my grandmother the money he had raised – after deductions that is, but she knew nothing about them.

'There's the fifteen bob, like I said.' He gave us six shiny half-crowns – two apiece – and said, 'It's been nice doin' business with you,' like a real businessman would.

'It's been nice doin' business with you,' we each said in turn and shook the gentleman's hand.

When the policeman came our parlour was in playtime – quarter to five of an evening – and Billy and I were doing a jigsaw puzzle on the parlour table. The policeman said that he wanted to see Mr Brown and my grandmother fetched him from Mr Doyle's piggery.

'It's about some suits which tha's pawned in Castleford,' the policeman said, holding his helmet under his arm. He was only a young constable and he shuffled uncomfortably at what he was about to say. 'Savoy Hotel, eh?' He looked at Mr Brown's shabby trousers and at his dirty striped shirt. 'When was thee ever at the Savoy Hotel in London?'

'About ten years sin,' Mr Brown answered. 'I used to go regular when I was sellin' me paper bags.' He winked at Billy and me.

'Tha's sure tha's not bin more recent?'

'No.' Our lodger shook his head.

'Then how come tha's pawning clothes with Savoy hangers on 'em?'

'What's this all about?' asked Mr Brown. 'I'll not answer any more of tha questions unless th' explains thasen.'

'Just answer my question, please,' said the constable.

'No. What's going on? What's tha suggestin'?'

'There's been a theft, Mr Brown. Someone cleaned out the wardrobes from a number of rooms at the Savoy Hotel in London a few years since and tha's got spankin' new clothes pawned on Savoy hangers. How does th' explain that?'

'They was my suit and others' Sunday best who live 'ere and I found the hangers, that's how I explain it, constable. Now if tha'll excuse me I'll get back to t' pigs.'

'Well, where d'tha find the hangers, Mr Brown?'

The lodger looked at Billy and me for a moment then he coughed loudly and spat a black gobbet on the fire. When he turned he continued to look at Billy then he said, 'Found 'em on a tree.'

'Where?' said the policeman.

Mr Brown looked now at me concentrating his eyes on my lips. I was mouthing the words silently, willing him to understand.

'Aken Jugs,' he eventually said.

'Tha expects me to believe that tha found coat hangers from the Savoy Hotel in London on a tree at Aken Jugs?'

'Ay, I do,' he said.

'Yes, he does,' I piped up.

'Now, son, no need to go tellin' stories for the likes of Mr Brown. We know all about Mr Brown in Castleford, don't we, Mr Brown?'

'What's tha mean?' my grandmother asked.

'Nothing, Mrs Brightside. Just that we know all about Mr Brown's previous activities. Now, come on, Mr Brown, tha'd better come down to the police station with me and tha can mek a statement there.'

We watched with horror as the policeman slapped handcuffs on to Mr Brown's wrists and frog-marched him out of the house. Billy and I ran after them as my grandmother plonked herself heavily into a chair.

'It weren't him. It was Billy and me. We took the hangers,' I shouted.

The constable smiled as he escorted our lodger over the common, leading him by the arm. Mr Brown looked at me and he said, 'Best say nowt, lad. Go back home. I'll see thee soon.' He didn't come home that night.

I lay awake hearing the voices thrown up by the dark tide of night which had engulfed us. I no longer slept in my parents' bed but alone in a small bed at their side.

Get tha bloody foot off my pipe.

It's not on tha pipe.

It is, tha's not letting watter thru.

I'm not on tha bloody pipe. Tha must be standing on th' own bloody pipe.

'Rube Hardwick,' I said. 'Rube, tha's standing on his pipe.'

It's not Rube, it's me.

'Who? Mr Brown?'

No, Mr Brown's in jail. It's me.

'Who's me when tha's at home?'

It's me, tha brother, daft.

'I haven't got a brother,' I said aloud and I sat up in my bed, sweat pouring from my brow. The stones were speaking, bringing the madness which they had inflicted upon my great aunt Henrietta – or so I thought.

7

*My mother, Mary Brightside, and the moment she
knew who she was*

My mother's story cannot be told without also revealing the conflict which circled within her, which was eventually to eddy up in me, which there was in our family after her marriage to William Brightside and which remained a constancy in daily village life. In its widest dimension it was the struggle between capital and labour, the coal owner and the pitmen. With regard to myself, it was typified by the opposing views I had of my two grandfathers: Ernest, the one with whom I lived and loved, and Joseph Thwaite, the one who lived at the big house less than a mile away yet was as remote as the King of England. As for my mother, it was the tension created in being both the daughter of the coal owner and the wife of a collier – and it was a tension which, no matter how it may appear to have been controlled, was constantly revolving within her slender frame.

Don't get me wrong, after her marriage and following my birth my mother had no loyalty to the Thwaites – her loyalties lay squarely with the Brightsides and in the Brightside home. It was other people who shifted the focus of her tensions, circling it about at their pleasure as if it was a wheel fixed to the cam which they controlled. They could poke it at her as they would a stick and my mother's wheel would find itself elsewhere, somewhere she never intended it to be, and as with all things poked at the ends of sticks she suffered a mixture of anger and fear. It was the geography of the place to which she was pushed that frightened her, for it was always that she found herself on the edge. She was never pushed over the edge, never banished properly, she was just kept at bay and found herself walking the dangerous perimeters of circles.

She had been brought up to be a lady, the granddaughter of old Thwaite, the one who had sunk the shaft and built the terrace of houses long, long ago. Old Thwaite, because at a time even before the sinking of the shaft he had been a pitman, had some sympathy with the miners – he knew their needs and though he had a reputation for being a hard man he wouldn't often see his workers starve. He knew the politics of the pit instinctively and he would always skilfully negotiate to firstly keep the pit productive, that was paramount – if he wasn't producing coal nobody won. But secondly he would negotiate production at a rate which gave employment to a maximum number of bodies at a wage where the least number might starve. He was a hard man but he wasn't a wicked man. Not like his son, Joseph, who locked out the men whenever the fancy took him.

Mary was brought up at the big house and as a child had played in the gardens among the warm sad trees. The gardens were bounded by a high wall which had a single set of gates. They had big stone pillars at either side and there were great stone pineapples on top of the pillars which everyone thought were just fancy balls until the coming of the cinema – then after seeing the film about East Africa we all learned that they were pineapples. I suppose that my mother knew they were pineapples long before my father did. He had to wait for the cinema, she had a governess. So my mother from an early age knew all sorts of things and spoke properly. She was pretty too. My father told me that she was the prettiest thing that he had ever seen. When he first set eyes on her she was playing on the red painted swing, in the gardens at the big house with her brothers and her sisters. They were both then fifteen years old. He had heard about her – he had heard about all of the Thwaite children – but he had not seen them until that day. Mary had a straw boater on her head like the one which Henrietta sometimes wore and she had on a long blue dress

91

with something shiny threaded into the material and it shone and dazzled him in the sunshine.

'What do you want?' one of her brothers asked as William walked down the path among the weeping trees. The foliage pressed upon him causing an unease never expressed in nature beyond that walled place.

'Ah've come to see Mr Thwaite. I brought 'im summat from my father.'

'Oh, well, I suppose you'd better go knock on the door then, but go around the back, don't go to the front door for heaven's sake.' William knew that the girl on the swing was staring at him but when he turned his face to hers she looked away from his dirty and torn breeches at which she had been staring. My mother gazed without concern into the sun and my father continued on his uncertain path to the house. He had never seen it before, not close up. He counted fifteen windows on the flat-fronted façade. Three rows of five windows – and he wondered which one would belong to the room of the pretty girl on the swing. In fact it was none of them; Mary slept at the back of the house which had just as many windows set into its dismal stone. As he approached within feet of the front door looking for a path which might take him round to the back of the house as the boy had suggested, the door opened and Thwaite came out with two dogs heaving at chokers about their heavy throats. William was frightened.

'What's tha want, lad?'

'Ah wants Mr Thwaite, sir.'

'Well, tha's got 'im. Stand still and the dogs'll not harm thee.'

'My father asked me to give thee this, Mr Thwaite.'

'Oh, ay. Who's tha father, when he's at 'ome?' he said, taking the package from William.

'Mr Brightside.'

'Ernest Brightside?'

'Ay.'

'I knew tha great grandfather, lad. John. John, wasn't it?'

'Yes.'

'Ay. John. I knew John. I worked in pit with John and tha great grandmother, Jane.'

'Yes, Mr Thwaite.'

'Worked with 'er, too. Still here, isn't she?' And whilst William nodded he said, 'Give tha great grandmother my regards, lad.'

'Yes, sir.'

'Tell tha father,' he said and he raised in the air the parcel which William had given him and waved it above the silk hat on his head, but he never said what it was that he should tell his father. Just 'Tell tha father,' that's all he said, waving the parcel about. As the dogs barked my father watched the sky turning blue all about the head of the black-clad coal owner.

'Yes, Mr Thwaite.'

As he turned to leave, the dogs growled angrily at his movement and strained all the more to be free of the leash. Old Thwaite said, 'It's all right, lad, I've got 'em. Tha'd better run whilst tha can,' and my father hared off as quickly as he could go, back through the green pressing trees to the other side of the gates with the pineapple balls.

He went back every day to see the girl on the red swing but usually she wasn't about. Once or twice he caught sight of her playing in the gardens and he would creep into the bushes and watch her from the sadness of the lush leaves. He would never reveal himself, though, not because he was uncertain of what she might say or because he was ashamed of his dirty dress but out of fear of the dogs. One of those dogs might have taken a piece out of his arse as large as a rich man's dinner. Then one day my father had the idea of taking Bruno, the Bellman's dog, with him on one of his visits to the big house. It was with blind faith that he said to Bruno, 'Now look, Bruno, we're off to seek the lass who lives with Mr Thwaite and if we can find her tha's got to help me. There's two big brutes who live up there in the big house and I know tha's not a lass thasen, Bruno, but

93

does tha think tha could tek 'em off somewheres whilst I talk to the girl? Does tha think tha can find some way of occupying their attention or summat?'

Bruno just looked at my father with his intelligent brown eyes and whilst Bruno didn't have the same effect on William as he would later have on me, he knew that Bruno had understood and that he would help my father if he could. They went up to the big house and hid in the bushes together and waited for the girl to eventually appear. She sat alone on the red swing lazily twisting and untwisting in the heat and my father asked Bruno to go into the gardens and find the two big dogs and to take them off as he had agreed he would.

Bruno ambled on to the lawns and barked at the girl on the swing. She took no notice of him. So Bruno sat on the lawn shuffling his bottom on the grass and barked at the house with his black back to the girl. There was a barked response from within and soon the two great brutes came flying from the front door and raced up to the Bellman's dog, growling and barking as if they intended to tear off his head. Bruno sat becalmed in the centre of the lawn and barked at the sky, ignoring the two who had just appeared. Then they both sniffed at him but he refused to budge and remained sitting on his bottom. One of them had his nose rooted beneath Bruno's tail but the black dog still refused to budge; he continued to bark into the sky as if he were telling it to come down and do something. But the sky just sat up there and Bruno continued pluckily to sit on the lawn, now with both of the coal owner's dogs rooting together and trying to lift him out of the ground like a claw hammer eases an old nail from a bit of wood. But Bruno had his solid tail anchored firmly to the lawn and still refused to budge. By now the others had ceased their barking and alternated their attention between Bruno's seated rear end and his barking head which was still fixed on the sky. Suddenly the black dog got up and walked off down the path, the others docilely following him, and my father saw him take them out beyond the gates and into the world of the miners. Then my father shouted, 'Ay up' and he threw a small stone at my mother which hit her on the ankle. She turned to see the boy who had delivered the parcel to her grandfather two weeks before. He was half submerged in the bushes and he made gestures with his hands calling her to him. She left the swing twirling in the lazy afternoon light and approached the boy.

'What's tha name?' he asked her, bending down so that he was out of sight of anyone at the house.

'Mary. What's yours?'

'William.' He didn't know what else to say and became embarrassed. 'Tha grandfather and my great grandfather were friends,' he told her eventually in an uncertain voice. She looked at him, smiling but unable to think of how she should reply. 'Can we be friends like them?' he eventually asked her.

'I don't know,' she told him.

'Well, can I come here again just to see thee, like? Can I see thee here in t'garden again?'

'I suppose it will be all right.'

The front door to the big house opened and somebody whistled for the dogs. Then, when they hadn't responded, the person in the doorway started shouting Mary's name over and over again and she told my father that she had to go indoors but that she would like to see him again sometime, just to say hello in the garden like they did now, and she left him alone in the warm secret of the bushes. He returned home in a daze, his heart thumping and the blood flushing up his cheeks. The dogs too returned to the big house. They went home each with several teeth missing. Bruno had been showing them how to play cricket on the common with the lads.

My father and Bruno went back to the big house on many occasions after that and Bruno always took the dogs off to some exciting new place. He taught them to swim down at Bottom Boat and he showed them the old mine where my great grandfather had found the dinosaur and where he was buried under the collapsed skeleton. He led them to the church in the next village to show them where God was and he showed them the ashpits behind our terrace of smoking houses. They were never the same after that – Bruno had brought down the sky and civilised them. The world was now a smaller, more friendly place and they weren't brutes any longer; after a time my father had no need to take Bruno with him when he went up to the big house for the two dogs became his friends. Whenever he rustled in the bushes they would bark and someone would let them out of the house and they would come lolloping over to him and lick his face with a true affection.

Then one day old Thwaite discovered him sitting in the bushes with his granddaughter; the two dogs were lying beside them flicking flies with their lazy tails and watching them kiss. The mine owner raved and ranted and chased my father from his property and threatened to have the Brightside family evicted from their home, because that was his property as well. Then he had the dogs put down and replaced them with two more brutes who tore up rabbits and even sheep with their big jaws. Mary began to dislike her grandfather after that and sometimes, not very often, but sometimes when it was possible for her to get away she met William under the gas lamp on the common and they would go over to Hunger Hill to do their courting. Then when Elyahou Tsiblitz brought the washable condoms to our village, like so many other curious couples married or not, they made love in a starry haze of coal dust which on some nights had the habit of glittering the air like green diamonds causing babies to come from nowhere, penetrate the rubber sheaths and swell the bellies of the leggy lasses.

That was how I came to be and how my mother and father came to be married. Old Thwaite didn't like it but when they named me Donald after him, and when he learned that I had his same mischievous blue eyes, he relented and at least he came to see me and cried on my mother's shoulder. Grandfather Joseph, however, didn't have his father's softness and he cut my mother from the family without a penny. Her father had not spoken to her since before I was born. It was harsh, then, that some of our neighbours would not speak with her either. As I said, they held her at arm's length with sticks as if she was a different animal, and she didn't know where she belonged. Emily knew though, Emily quite rightly said that she belonged with the Brightsides, and that's where she stayed till she died. But she did walk those outer circles when she wasn't at home – the suspicion of some of the less pleasant of our neighbours pushing her there.

I can't remember exactly when it was, but there was a time after the bringing of the electricity that I heard it gather momentum on Hunger Hill. It ran ever so fast in the wires, scorching the moss and burning up the grass. It hummed very loudly at night. The extra surge caused our parlours to glow with so much candle power that when viewed from across the common the rooms seemed to be bathed in a startling brightness. We sat for a time in a kind of naked explosion, listening to our electric wirelesses and ironing our long johns. It disturbed us. It made the women self-conscious and brought a variety of shades to cover the neat bulbs and a selection of curtains to drape across the windows of the terrace, but even then the sheen glowed through. It was on such an evening during this period that young Doctor Cartwright informed my mother that she was having twins and he told her not to be so surprised because twin births ran in the family. It was at that moment that my mother learned for sure that she was a Brightside for the Thwaites had nothing like that to offer to the world. They had only dogs which didn't know where the sky was and a head of family so cruel that he didn't need to sleep. They didn't have twins or anything as human as that.

8

The rediscovery of Bresci's hat

Ernest's condition worsened; he got himself all bent up and had difficulty in straightening his back, besides which the joints in his fingers swelled up and he could hardly move his hands. Young Doctor Cartwright advised him to go to bed, lie flat on his stomach and have weights applied to his spine and to the backs of his hands in an attempt to unbend them. He lay on his bed, naked to the waist, with a flat iron in the middle of his back and with weights from our baking scales holding down his fingers. Also, because young Doctor Cartwright had suggested that the presence of copper might help, Emily had piled pennies, halfpennies and farthing pieces along his spine and Lancaster had unwound the inductance from Mr Brown's crystal set and turned the copper wire about my grandfather's wrists. He was given an aspirin tablet with a glass of water every three hours. After a day or two of such treatment Ernest told Emily that his back felt a lot better and she removed the weights. She also took the weights from his hands but she left the copper wire binding up his wrists and rewound it a little around his fingers too. There were great swellings on his joints. It was just as well that he was locked out, she told him, for with his hands in such a state he would never have been able to have held the pick.

He heard the Bellman come to the village and climbed clumsily from his bed. He thrust up the window in my parents' bedroom using the backs of his hands and he put his greying head into the dull day. A crowd larger than normal had assembled to hear the Bellman's news – everyone was waiting on news of Mr Brown.

'They've gone and stuck him away for six months,' Jacky told us.

'But 'e didn't do owt,' Ernest said from the window. Billy and I had told my grandfather what we knew about the hangers.

'Oh, ay, 'e did,' said Jacky.

'What?' said my grandfather. 'What did he do?' The eyes of the crowd were on my grandfather leaning painfully from the window.

''E stole 'em.'

'What? I don't believe it,' said my grandfather. 'Why should he go and steal a load of coat hangers?'

'Not the hangers. It weren't the hangers he was done for – it was the paper bags.'

'What! All them paper bags he was forever blowin' into?'

'Ay. 'E stole 'em from the bag factory in York, tha naws.'

'When was this?' asked my grandfather, who liked to know the sequence of things before he could accept a judgement.

''E stole some only last week. Apparently 'e were allus doin' it. Compulsive, the magistrate said 'e was. A compulsive thiever of paper bags. Brown ones. Like 'is name.'

I couldn't believe what we were being told. 'No,' I shouted up, 'Mr Brown had his own factory. He made his own paper bags, Mr Jellis.'

'Oh, ay, an' I got a place making jam sandwiches,' said Mr Archbold, who had slung up his bedroom window only a short distance from where my grandfather's naked torso leaned into the daylight. Everyone laughed. I felt ashamed that I had piped up when I had.

'Never mind, son,' Jacky said kindly. 'We all get took in from time to time.' Then to all the others he said, 'It weren't his first conviction for it. It was third time 'e'd bin copped for stealing paper bags. Police'll be comin' o'er to tha 'ouse, Ernest,' he then called up to my grandfather. ''Appen they'll be searchin' for the bags.'

99

I broke into a cold sweat and saw that Billy had turned bright pink.

'We'll ave to be rid of 'em,' my friend informed me in a quiet voice.

We went down to Owler Crimble to find Isaac. He would know what to do. When we found him the lad was sitting on a log and had fallen fast asleep with the wooden clapper across his knee.

'We'll 'ave to burn 'em,' Billy told him when the boy had woken up and we had told him of the stolen loot which was stashed in our hut.

'Int no point in doin' that,' he said. 'Tha's just mekin' a panic for nowt. We can tek 'em o'er to my father. They'll hide in his desk until it's forgotten, nobody ever think of lookin' there.' Isaac was ice cool. A welcome influence on our overheating brains.

'Come on,' he said. 'We'll go get 'em now.'

We walked across to the hut and Isaac stuffed the bags down his trousers and told us that he would take them to his father's house.

The following day the lock-out ended. Thwaite had sold all his coal to a gentleman in India and informed us that we didn't have to take a cut in wages after all. In fact he gave each man another sixpence per shift and my family went back to the pit tapping out a little more than normal. Emily bought more pot ducks for the wall in the parlour to show the neighbours how affluent we were.

Of the few visitors who regularly came to our house the one I didn't tell you about was the man from the Burial Society. He came every Tuesday evening. His name was Mr Willmott and he came on a bicycle. His tash grew so low over his mouth that when he spoke you couldn't see his lips moving and I used to wonder if it was he who had spoken at all. The words didn't even come from his direction. He would sit very still at the parlour table with a money bag in

100

his hands and with cycle clips about the bottoms of his trousers. He was only animated when it was time to drop the pennies which my grandfather had just given him into the bag. Then he would nod his long head for a moment or two and stare at my grandfather with dark smouldering eyes. Billy said that he was a Martian and that his eyes were capable of emitting a ray that could pierce metal. He always wore a neat collar which was buttoned down with little brass studs and he had a red tie. Throughout the time of his visit he would just sit and apparently not say anything. Ernest always looked as if he was having a conversation with someone else when Mr Willmott came. It was as if there were three people in the room – Mr Willmott, my grandfather and a third person. Someone over there, whom you never saw.

Ernest paid into the Burial Society because Emily insisted that he should. He paid the insurance for all of us, even for Mr Brown and even during the six-month period the lodger spent in jail. The money, though it wasn't a lot, could have been used for the purchase of food but Emily insisted that when the time came we all had to be decently put away. A pauper's grave would have been ignominious and she would never have had the neighbours see us in such a disgrace. Our deaths, like our Sunday suits, were going to confer a respect upon us. We could walk tall, happy in the knowledge that self-esteem would follow even after the destruction of self. The effect of such tortuous thought was to give me a headache. Such questions needed the mind of a philosopher, so I went outside and asked my duck if self-esteem was practised by the spirits. He promptly turned himself upside down and showed me his arse. He refused to reappear until I had gone back indoors and seated myself with my grandfather, who as always was admiring the strange ventriloquism of Mr Willmott. I looked back out of the parlour window. My duck was asleep on the still surface of his rain barrel water.

When my great great grandmother died she had a grand

funeral. There were four black horses, each with red and white plumes, which dragged her carriage away from the dark stone of the terrace house and up the hill to the church in the next village. There were motor cars and carriages following and my father started up the Jam Sahib's motor and I rode with him and my mother among the cortège. I remember looking back. 'Don't look back,' my mother said. 'It's unlucky.' But I looked back and saw hundreds of people in their best clothes all following the coffin up the hill, their flat caps jostling under a thin rain. Then my father looked back with tears in his eyes and eventually my mother turned her head too. She never instructed me not to look back again.

When she went, my great great grandmother had left a fortune hidden somewhere. It was the fortune which she was reputed to have brought with her after her husband had died and when she came to live at our house. Some of it had been spent – the cameras which she had bought for Lancaster and Albert and all of those painting materials which she had given them to launch their artists' careers. That must have cost. There had been many other presents, too, not to mention the money she had handed over in payment for the Jam Sahib's motor. But the general feeling was that there was more, much more – but nobody knew where it was. There is a photograph in our family album which had been taken by Albert. It is a photograph of the old woman standing on Hunger Hill and she is seen to be nursing a large suitcase in her arms. She has a cap on her head. The cap is commonly believed to be that of Bresci, the man who assassinated the King of Italy and the brother-in-law of Uncle Elyahou Tsiblitz. His former wife's brother's hat, that is. The suitcase is commonly believed to contain the missing fortune but, as I told you, nobody knows where it is. Albert spent a lot of effort digging about the summit of Hunger Hill, which is where the photograph was taken, but he didn't find anything. Then he just dug holes at random all about the village but he only succeeded in creating puddles of metal-tasting rain. Earlier still, the five Gill boys who had been our next-door neighbours had dug up the inside of our house when no one was at home, but they had found nothing either. So when my uncle Albert was found dead down the pit with Bresci's hat on his head it was assumed that he must have found the missing fortune. Of course, we didn't know that it was Bresci's hat, not at first anyway.

Ernest came home with his mates, he was all doubled up with his arthritis and he was crying. He opened the street door and came into the parlour, letting the yellow electric light escape from the house a little, and his mates waited outside huddled in its paleness. He explained to my grandmother that Albert was dead and that he didn't know how it had happened and she ran off upstairs to consider her grief. My mother went after her. It didn't do to be alone with grief; like a man from the asylum, there was no telling what it might do. Ernest dispatched Lancaster to go and tell Rosanne what had happened and to fetch her to the house because that's where they would bring the body when it was taken from the pit. My father was sent to get young Doctor Cartwright.

When the doctor arrived, Albert's body was already laid out on the parlour table. Rosanne had been taken off to join my grandmother in the bedroom and Clarrie sat on her grandfather's knee, unable to understand why her father wouldn't wake up. It was a reasonable lack of understanding, Albert did appear to be asleep. Asleep in his grimy clothes and with a dirty face and with a flat cap on his head. Lancaster was trying to remove the cap from his dead brother's head but it wouldn't come off. He complained immediately and somewhat vaguely to Doctor Cartwright that he was unable to remove the cap from Albert's head and the doctor concluded that Lancaster was in a state of shock and made him sit down. Mrs Gill, who had come from next door, gave him some strong tea. The doctor then tried to remove it but he too was unable to wrench the cap away. Our neighbours, some of whom were staring in at the window, were now shouting advice on how best to be rid of the hat, advocating in turn the use of Mr Doyle's lard and a good lathering of glycerine of soap on the forehead of the deceased.

Then my grandfather, handing Clarrie on to me, said, 'Give it 'ere,' and tried to get his fingers under the cap so that he could lift it from his son's head, but he couldn't control his arthritic fingers. His swollen nodules were too large and too painful to allow him to get his fingers between the cap and Albert's head and the neighbours then advised smearing his fingers with Vaseline. Ernest put his head into his curled-up hands and wept with frustration.

Finally, Emily came down the rickety stairs, my mother hanging on to her elbow. My grandmother immediately closed the curtain across the window and over the startled faces of the onlookers. She kissed her son's dirty face and asked my mother to put some hot water into a bowl and to bring her a rag. Whilst all about hopelessly watched she took a pair of scissors from the drawer directly beneath the bible in the sideboard and cut the cap at the side of Albert's head, close by his dead ear. The cap then came away and she handed it to Ernest. There was a clean white ring about my uncle's forehead. Then she bathed his face whilst my mother knelt beside her holding the bowl of steaming water. She washed away all the coal dust and kissed him again, this time on both cheeks. Then she straightened up and faced my grandfather.

'How did it happen?' she asked her husband almost as if it was he who had been responsible.

'I dunno,' Ernest shrugged whilst squeezing the cap in his two arthritic hands. 'Archbold comes to me just before the end of the shift and 'e says, "It's tha lad, Ernest. Tha'd better go and see." And 'e was there in the gallery lying on 'is face when I went to look.' His chest trembled and wheezed and I saw my grandfather's face all screwed up and tears squeezed from his eyes. Then he stood for ages, trembling and looking at his dead son laid on the table, and nobody seemed to know what to do.

'Stinking pit,' was all that my grandmother said and she sat heavily down into a wide winged chair.

The doctor started to examine the body. Then Rosanne came downstairs and clutched Clarrie to her. After his examination the doctor said, 'I can't find anything wrong. Seems like natural causes.'

'What tha mean, like his heart or summat?' Ernest asked.

'Maybe,' said the doctor and he watched Ernest turning the hat in his hands. 'Had he complained of feeling ill?' he asked Rosanne and she shook her fair head.

Then quite suddenly my grandfather, who had been turning the hat inside out and back again several times, said, 'Hang on. This is my cap. This is the cap that grandmother gave me, the one which Bill Pettit told us had belonged to the man who killed the King of Italy.'

Everyone then seemed to lose interest in the corpse.

'Give it 'ere, Father,' said William. 'Ay. 'Tis,' he said. 'Look 'ere, it's got 'is name in it. Gaetano Bresci,' he told all who were assembled in the parlour.

'Well I nivver,' said my grandfather, as if now nothing had happened to his son other than that he had found a long-lost hat.

'Tha naws what this means, doesn't tha, Father?' Lancaster said, dashing to the bookshelf and turning up the photograph which Albert had taken. 'There,' he said, pointing to the hat which Great Great Grandmother had worn on that day. 'It's the same hat.'

'Albert found the bloody fortune,' William told my grandfather, light dawning all over his face.

Rosanne insisted that the wagon be used as a funeral carriage. She wished that she had still got the shire horse to pull it – Albert would have liked that, she said – but she was more than satisfied when the Burial Society offered the four black horses with the red and white plumes to pull the wagon. We all went in a procession up the hill to the church in the next village.

Ernest ranted. He was a lay preacher and he had picked up the ranter's ways. My great great grandmother would have hated it, having to listen to her Ernest going on about poverty and punishment and how we all should behave ourselves and accept what the Lord sends us or we would be packed off to everlasting damnation. He went on about resurrections as if it was Easter and at one time seemed to be talking about the resurrection of his son. It became all too much for my grandmother.

'Ernest,' she told him, 'sit thasen down. Stop frightenin' thasen and everone else with tha nonsense. Albert's gone and tha'll not bring him home with that sort of talk. Why he died God alone knows, but it's all to do with the grim funny business of life, Ernest, and it's about time tha learned such a thing. The grim funny business of life will get us all in the end. So don't go mekin' such a fuss, luv.' Then she sat down and sniffed into her handkerchief. The congregation sat for a while in stunned silence whilst the four plumed horses stood quietly in the warm sunshine beyond the open door, not doing much other than occasionally move their legs away from the blowflies. They made distinct clopping noises that echoed in the silent pews. One of them did his droppings on the path in front of the doors. Then we all went out and buried our Albert. We had a tea at our house and people kept coming in and they said how sorry they were that Albert had gone whilst they ate my grandmother's jam tarts. 'Yes, I'm sorry he's gone too, luv,' is just about all she would say to anybody.

At about six o'clock somebody asked where Rosanne and Clarrie were and though we searched about we couldn't find them. Then Billy o' the Terrus End pointed out that the wagon had gone. We all ran outside. I could never remember before having seen the gas lamp without the red and gold wagon parked under it. I felt that something had gone from my life. Then Mr Piggott came over and told my grandfather that he had seen the wagon being pulled by the four plumed horses on the Wakefield road. He had passed them in his car only half an hour before. He said that Rosanne was up at the front and that she had a long whip with which she lashed the horses like a madwoman.

'Never mind,' my grandfather said. 'She has her own grief to live with.'

It wasn't until a couple of days later that we realised that she had gone off with the Burial Society's prize horses.

'Well, somebody's at last got more than a burial out of 'em,' my father commented sarcastically.

A few days after that we realised that Rosanne had probably scarpered with Great Great Grandmother's fortune too.

It wasn't long before we had another funeral to attend. It was the burial of my little brother who had to be put into a pauper's grave as no one had ever paid subscriptions into a Burial Society for the little fellow. My grandmother told Mr Willmott that it was all a piece of nonsense, since no one would ever think about someone being dead before they were born. Mr Willmott didn't say anything, at least I don't think that he said anything, he just continued to stare at her with his piercing eyes and she asked him if it was possible to transfer payments from one name to another. But the insurance man was adamant that burial insurance could only be for named individuals in the policy, unless you were to take out another policy to cover those persons who might not have a name. He explained that if the family had taken out such a policy then my brother would have most certainly been covered – providing my mother's pregnancy had gone full term. If it hadn't, then there would have had to have been a third policy to cover him because he wouldn't have been classed as a person – just an embryo or something.

The twins had been born. There was a boy and a girl but the boy had been born dead. He was tiny, like Lancaster had been when he was born. The girl was a great bouncy thing and Doctor Cartwright said that it was probable that, just as was the case with Lancaster and Albert, the girl had been standing on the boy's umbilical and had cut off his nourishment; but where Lancaster had survived, my brother unfortunately had not. Mr Brown returned just in time to attend the funeral. My sister was christened Irene Rose and Henrietta sent her a rubber cot sheet from Berlin.

9

Significant events inside an onion

In 1919 Lloyd George set up a Royal Commission of Enquiry into the state of the mining industry, telling the miners that he would implement whatever recommendations were made, but at the same time assuring his cabinet that the Commission wasn't likely to suggest any radical changes. He told his colleagues that even if the Commission were to recommend nationalisation, a very radical change but a most unlikely proposal, then he would not be prepared to pass the necessary legislation. Well, the Royal Commission went and recommended nationalisation, didn't it, and old Lloyd George had to break his pledge to the miners. Of course, Lloyd George said that there never had been such a pledge; the implementation of their recommendations had been dependent on the Royal Commission's unanimity, he said, and as they were not unanimous there could be no nationalisation – the majority decision was neither here nor there.

The rumbling trouble in our village over the next twenty years had its roots in Lloyd George's broken pledge. All those strikes and lock-outs, ostensibly about rises in wages and cuts in wages and increased working hours, were really about the broken pledge. It was a measure of the miners' dislike for a man who had shown himself at some time a hero only to settle to being a plain cheat. Everyone got very confused about the issues after that and even the union lost sight of what the discontent was about. At one time it had been about 'Mines for the Nation' and then suddenly it was about wages and working conditions. But it wasn't, it wasn't about wages and conditions at all. In our village it was about being rid of Thwaite. As long as Thwaite remained the coal owner the troubles would rumble on.

Working people had talked about a General Strike for a century or more but when it came it really was a non-event. It lasted only nine days, yet fifty years later people spoke of it as if it was the most significant thing in modern British history. In the first place our village had been locked out for months before the event – it was called in our support anyway – and we were to be strike-bound for many months after it was all over. So for us it was nine days of nothing in the middle of a much greater period of inaction. The year was like an onion, it had layers. At either end was a month or so of work. The rest of the months were either locked out or strike-bound and in the dead centre were those nine days in May when the nation stood still. It was during that period of doing nowt in 1926 that significant things happened in our village.

Lancaster, going on seven years home from the War, had still not managed to shake himself free from the past. The war years tugged at him, pulling him continually back to the terror of the skies. His dead comrades limped by. His dead relatives and friends, those whom he hadn't properly mourned, constantly called him. He wanted to go. He wanted to follow Archie Jellis and Bruno down to London but ghosts kept on calling him back. Then one day in the middle of the General Strike Lancaster got up from the chair in which he slept and shaved as always in the scullery. In the small mirror which hung on a piece of bent wire and dangled from the window frame behind the sink he saw the street door closing behind him. There was only himself imaged in the glass and he started to whistle an old song. He took himself off to the schoolhouse. On the way he could hear Isaac's father potting at the pigeons and the rooks with his shotgun. At the school he asked Wenceslas Piggott if he could finish off Albert's painting on the wall at the back of Standard One.

Slowly, and disappointingly for the children, the two shadowy figures seated on the bed were transformed from curved, full-breasted symbols of sketchy voluptuousness into a likeness of the craggy and handsome reality of my twin uncles attired in a strange Sunday best. Flights of fancy gave them neat clean collars and striped ties and brought to one of them a pair of angel's wings. The one without the wings unaccountably wore my grandparents' glasses and held a white cane like a blind man might have done. The two figures perched at the edge of the bed dressed in their electric blue best appeared to be slightly nervous of their surroundings in a very ordinary room. I guessed that the one with the wings was my uncle Albert but Lancaster would never tell which was whom.

Mr Brown said that in finishing Albert's painting, Lancaster had taken on his twinly duty of having to tie up his brother's loose ends. Settling his estate, he called it. Young Doctor Cartwright, looking into the schoolroom through the closed dirty window and seeing Lancaster sitting on the top of Mr Clayton's steps at the back of Standard One, agreed that he was certainly tying up loose ends for he saw it that my uncle was knotting the umbilical.

'Surely tha does that after a man's birth, not after his death,' Mr Brown told him uncertainly, for he didn't like to be questioning the doctor's province: Doctor Cartwright delivered most of the babies born into our village these days.

'Not necessarily,' the doctor pontificated. 'In the case of twins, twins like these two, there is a second umbilical which needs attention. The rope which ties them together throughout their lives needs attention too. There comes a time when that must be severed, you see. Lancaster hardly wants to be dragging his brother's corpse about with him for the rest of his life, does he? So he tidies up the estate like you say, Mr Brown, and then he snips the cord and lets his brother sail free.'

Mr Brown looked into the sky as if at any moment Doctor Cartwright might have Albert floating there. 'What of Irene

Rose?' he then asked the doctor, bringing his lonely gaze back to earth.

'The lad had no estate, Mr Brown,' the doctor reminded him and left hurriedly to call on his next patient.

The day that H. G. Wells stole Marlene Jellis from the pub, my uncle Lancaster, having tidied up his brother's estate, spoke to Mr Brown of talking pictures.

First things first. A turned signpost brought what little traffic there was down to the village. Most of it wandered about the common a while and then Billy o' the Terrus End directed the cars back up the hill from where they had come down, telling the motorists that they must be daft if they imagined that here was the way to Leeds. We watched them disappear into the distance by the big house, each motor giving a tired honk as it negotiated the steep rise. Then at about four o'clock a bull-nosed Morris arrived and the motorist dismounted at the far end of the terrace. He was dressed in a neat but very lengthy overcoat and he wore a trilby on his head. The man was all muffled up with a scarf so that one couldn't see his face. He smoked a Turkish cigarette which disappeared into the folds of material and presumably from there on into his mouth, which was completely hidden from view. The yellow smoke which curled from the lighted end of the cigarette hung about his head like an extra garment.

'Is there a public bar in the village?' he asked us without removing the cigarette. We could see now that he wore goggles beneath the scarf but we were unable to see the man's eyes.

Billy pointed. 'O'er yon,' he said and when the man had walked off in the direction of the pub he said excitedly, 'That's the invisible man, Donald. Did tha see?'

I watched the man walking away from us and heard his shoes squeaking. 'I'nt no such thing,' I told my friend, convinced somehow that squeaky shoes were something which one could only attribute to the material.

'He's a friend of Mr Willmott's,' Billy said, undeterred by my scepticism. 'He's been to Mars, tha naws, 'as the invisible man. Probably brought Willmott back with him, last time he went.' Then with a last edgy glance at the departing stranger he sneered, 'Who'd buy insurance from a Martian?'

I suddenly felt guilty for my family's support of the man from another planet. Commission for aliens was not something in which we were now encouraged to indulge. Things weren't like they had been in the days of Great Great Grandmother. She had encouraged a warmth for Elyahou Tsiblitz and it hadn't been difficult for our neighbours to respond – most of them. Strangers, though distrusted, were eventually taken in to the hearts of the people. Even Mr Ndolo, the first black man to come to the village, had been accepted warmly after he had demonstrated how he could eat fire and then turn himself into a beautiful princess. I suppose it was the War that must have started it – this dislike of strangers. It hadn't been like that before the War – there had been distrust but not dislike. Bill Pettit maybe, perhaps Bill had hated, but not the others. But I expect that it's normal to hate if you happen to be born before your time like Bill had been. The world must be a strange and frightening place if you can mislay things in your head.

Then when old Thwaite died along came Joseph Thwaite and we all saw the terrible way that he and those strangers at the big house would treat the colliers – there was a real hatred of Thwaite and what he represented for he was at the dead centre of our misery, or so we told ourselves. Looking back on it, perhaps it was the War which after all taught us to hate and the coal owner just happened to become a convenient focus for our feelings.

Thwaite was at the dead centre of those nine days, too, at the dead centre of an inactive ten months. He was at the centre of 1926 and at the centre of what seemed to be years of Brightside troubles on either side of the strike. We were

113

inside that dark shell, he and I. My maternal grandfather and I were in the centre of a dark egg, pressed in; it was a struggle within the coal, a struggle within the living history of the stone, as my great aunt Henrietta might have said. Many years later Henry Moore, who came from just down the road, would show me that struggle in his gravid, sculpted forms and he would show me the road out through the hole in my mother's belly. But for the time being I was locked tight within the coal, an embryo being brought to term for a delivery into the stinking pit.

'Shall we go and see?' I asked Billy as the stranger went from our view.

We followed him over to the pub and from the open doorway watched Rube Hardwick draw half a pint of beer which he set down in front of the man who even on his rough stool at the small iron table retained his invisibility. Although the Turkish cigarette was now much shorter, the yellow smoke still hung about his clothes. He began to unwind the scarf from about his head and we each shivered a little, anticipating the horribleness of the man's lack of substance. I'm not sure why – perhaps when he sat down the man's shoes had ceased their squeaking – but I was beginning to sympathise with Billy's wild fantasy.

The only other people in the pub at that time were Mr Piggott and Marlene, who were engaged in conversation at a table next to the newcomer. Marlene rocked her buttocks on the small stool, her red hair done up in its neat bun. She seemed to stop in mid-sentence, her fascination for the stranger's revealing of himself equal to our own. The scarf continued to unwind. Were we to see bandages about an incorporeal mummy? It was with great disappointment that we learned that the man had eyes beneath his motor-ing goggles and that he had moustaches as bushy as any which we had yet seen.

He saw Marlene's fascination with his extra-long scarf and we heard him introduce himself first to Wenceslas and then to Marlene, at whom he twinkled. He called himself

Sosthenes Smith. Marlene caught her breath. Billy and I could see her holding it in and we thought that she might be counting to see if she could beat some kind of record for not breathing. Her face reddened. The stranger said that he was a futurologist and told Marlene that she was going to get a big surprise because she was going on a journey. Wenceslas looked very unhappy. Marlene was breathing again now but her face was still very red. The stranger hoped that he wasn't being too indelicate when he told her that she had a liking for older men. The stranger sipped his beer and Mr Piggott, painfully aware of his greying head, seemed to grow more gloomy. His tash drooped and Marlene told him to remove the beer from it as it was dripping on her arm. He gloomily sucked at his tash. Then the stranger asked Wenceslas Piggott how he didn't know that there were men on Mars and Billy gave me a nudge under the ribs with his bony elbow. Wenceslas said that he didn't know, he couldn't know for sure, and the man called him a ditherer. Marlene beamed at the stranger and Mr Piggott fell into an even deeper depression. Then the man said that we should all in years to come probably end up looking like Martians; without any legs because we drove about in motors and with great big heads because our brains were bound to expand with all the knowledge that we should have to fill them with. Wenceslas started to say that he was a schoolteacher and that in his opinion there wasn't so much knowledge about that it could make heads grow and anyway in his experience most people weren't very much interested in education. Most boys spent the day dreaming about lasses, he said, and Billy, whose brain was by now large enough to accommodate both Martians and women, gave me another dig in the ribs. Marlene looked angrily at Wenceslas for having raised such a matter in front of a total stranger. The schoolteacher looked positively suicidal after that and drank down his beer as if it were some painful toxic potion.

Then Sosthenes Smith, seeing the look which had passed

between the lovers, begged his leave of them and apologised, hoping that he hadn't caused a row or anything, and he got up to go, beaming at the red-faced Marlene. He slipped on his goggles and wound the lengthy scarf back around his head, then he pushed his way roughly between Billy and me; we were still standing at the door. Marlene, making a lightning decision, came hustling by and she caught up with him by the motor. He invited her to hop into his bull-nosed Morris and Sosthenes Smith drove her away. He shouted back to Billy and me, 'Which is the way to Leeds, boys?' and Billy and I both pointed over to Hunger Hill, but Sosthenes Smith was more than a match for the likes of us for he turned the car round and headed out the way he had come in. Marlene was already letting her hair fall over her golden brooch even before they had got as far as the big house.

You know, there are some mornings when the sun has risen a deep red colour over the river at Bottom Boat. It catches in the waving poplars down by the river bank and it casts tinted shadows in the fields and on the hill and across the village. The particles of coal dust which fill the air get tinged purple and deep violet and they scatter the dark light like little prisms. Everything is given an edge of the rose-red hues, even the transparent wings of insects which bustle in the pink air. Dragonflies and bees, mayflies, tree wasps and beetles take in the redness. Gromwell, holly, ribwort and sorrel are touched by it and the little forget-me-not flowers and sauce-alone turn magenta. At Aken Jugs the oaks seem to be aflame and in the crimble, the elder bursting alone from the red mother earth takes a fire to its berries and leaves. Hunger Hill hides behind its treacherous purple veil and you can hear the songs of the corncrake and the redpole. The bean begins to flower and the larks sing miles above the land. In this May morning the lime and the sycamore and the beech trees start to leaf. And in the blood-red grass the drunks who have slept the night

116

in the fields like fallen scarecrows rouse themselves, perhaps trailing a last note or two of the carousel with which they had sung themselves to sleep – a long-gone cadence slipping easily on the mind. Lullabies. Lullaby Danny Pratt's father, who had limped breathless from the pub the night before, pulls his cap over his eyes so as not to see the yellow Haltica beetle creeping orange on his dirty sleeve. Then up, up in a windmill, whirl-arms wheeling towards the village and his irate wife.

It had been Danny Pratt's father who had one such morning smashed his way through our scullery door and slithered to the floor by our white sink, with several bottles of Great Great Grandmother's herbal mixtures which he had grabbed from the rows of dusty shelving. Drunk and drugged on Ipomoea and Arnica nut he slumped there; a bag of warped dreams. Young Doctor Cartwright had said that he should be sent to the asylum at Wakefield where he would have his brains wrung out but Mrs Pratt wouldn't allow it. So she just took him back to the field and left him among the thorns and the crowfoot. She left him there for days sleeping off his poisoned intoxication while the larks twittered morning and night. Then, another red morn he had picked himself up and dragged himself faltering of both step and breath back to the house which huddled somewhere in the middle of our terrace. The smoke curled from the chimney pot, the fire roared, the bread fried in the pan, his sons took themselves off to the pit. In his parlour Danny Pratt's father imagined the corpses in the trenches, imagined the gas wafting through, imagined the command to fix bayonets and he charged the stairs. Then he fell asleep in his own bed until Mrs Pratt came to wake him in the afternoon with a pot of tea and a kiss.

So this red morn too, Danny Pratt's father, with his cap over his eyes, stands uncertainly up, wheezing in the field of flowering beans. He thrashes about with his legs, he whirls his arms with purpose and finds somehow the direction he must travel to find his wife. 'Coming home,' he's

117

saying. 'I'm coming home.' At the same moment Isaac's father, ever ready to protect his crop, beans as well as corn, fires the shotgun which he holds. He fires the gun only, I am sure, to frighten him but he puts a hole clean through the poor man's pickled head. The rooks lift off in a dust, clattering into the blazing red sky.

Mr Clayton discovered the body the following day and he got Wenceslas Piggott and my uncle to help him carry it home to Mrs Pratt. And we all had to troop off to bury Lullaby Danny Pratt's father and sing him to sleep forever in the far corner of the graveyard at the church in the next village.

My uncle Lancaster and Mr Brown, standing outside the walls of Henrietta's laboratory, saw Marlene Jellis speeding off in the stranger's motor but thought nothing of it. Emily had told them Marlene was always speeding off with some-body, as long as he had trousers. They didn't doubt that the muffled man also wore trousers.

'There must be some way of getting them to talk,' my uncle said. Ever since he had first voiced his thought of talking pictures whilst lying in Mrs Cushman's bed he had dreamed of the possibility, but Lancaster was no engineer and could find no way of theorising the technicalities which the problem presented, besides which he had been bound up with thoughts of other things. The past hadn't until that morning, when he looked in his shaving mirror and saw it departing behind him, let him go. At last he was able to bring his thought to the inventor of the brown paper bag.

'Synchronicity. That's what tha wants,' Mr Brown told him.

'What's that?'

'It's the exact marriage of sight and sound. Tha's being synchronous when tha's talking, like. Watch my lips move, see. I can't help it, can I – it's reality.'

'So what?'

'So the only true method would be for us to put the sound on to the film.'

'I don't understand.'

'Well, if tha could get the wave pattern of the sound on to the film and have it read and translated back into sound as the film is being shown on the screen and if tha could at the same time amplify the sound, then the picture would be synchronous with the sound and the bloody thing would look like it's talking to thee, see.'

'Is that possible?'

'Ay. Nowt's impossible. It'd just cost a bloody fortune, that's all.'

'So what else?'

'Well, t'other way would be two separate systems. Tha meks tha picture and tha records tha sound on a wax disc and tha marries 'em up like.'

'Would that be expensive?'

'Naw, not really. Tha's got camera, I could knock summat up for sound.'

Before the General Strike was finished we had all piled into the Royal Picture Palace to watch the very first talking picture ever seen in England. The film makers synchronised their machines and a picture of Mr Brown appeared rather shakily on the screen. There was no amplification of the sound so we had to be very quiet to hear the man, dressed up in his Sunday best, saying rather scratchily and in a very posh squeak, 'I'm sovvy, I have no tile for God and all that stun. It give me the bib.' Then Mr Brown smiled, eyes twinkling, from the white flickering screen and his tash drooped at us for what seemed an eternity. We clapped and cheered and stamped our feet and the urchins whistled enthusiastically at the marvel which we had just witnessed, then the figure on the screen bowed like a real gentleman would and he waved at us like royalty.

'How did tha know to bow, Mr Brown?' I asked him as I stood by the man in the darkened auditorium. 'How did tha know tha'd get all them people clapping thee?'

119

'I just knew it, son, just knew that if I could be heard then I'd 'ave 'em clappin' me.'

'Mr Brown, tha's a genius,' I told the lodger, not for the first time.

Word soon got about that there was a minor miracle to be heard at the Royal. People came from miles about and paid good money to see Mr Brown talking on film. The sequence was so short that Mr Pinkofsky could have filled his cinema a dozen times a night but he showed it only twice nightly, choosing to incorporate the film into the regular programme. That way, he argued, the miracle had an even greater impact on those who saw it.

On the day that we buried Danny Pratt's father, the police arrested Isaac's father for his murder. I didn't see much of Isaac after that. It seemed that it was all right to mix with thieves like Mr Brown but one shouldn't become involved with those who are themselves tainted with the most unforgivable of sins. Even when it's a terrible accident, as Isaac's father always pleaded it was. That didn't save him, though, and they hanged him at Leeds jail the following year. Sometimes I used to wonder whatever happened to my brown paper bags but I never could find the right reason to go up to the farmhouse and ask for them back – it just didn't seem to be right to be finding reasons in such circumstances. Gradually I just forgot about the bags, as I forgot about Isaac too. I used to see him occasionally in the crimble, asleep with the clapper across his knee, but I didn't bother to waken him. I sometimes used to see his mother too, policing the beanfield with the shotgun beneath her arm and keeping it clear of the rooks and the pigeons. The killing hadn't deterred the drunks, though. They still flopped in the fields at night and woke up like scarecrows on rosy mornings.

The funeral brought its change in me, too. I stood about the graveside with all the others, hearing the wail of little Danny above the singing, and I thought of how beautiful was that word lullaby. I said it over to myself time and again until it became a foreign word devoid of any meaning. I broke the word into its three syllables and slowly repeated the three syllables to myself until it was all as incomprehensible as my uncle's painting at the back of Standard One. One could now only guess at the meaning. Then I suddenly said aloud, 'Lullaby Danny Pratt's father,' as if I had unlocked a door with a key which I didn't know that I possessed and all of the syllables lined up in tidy meaning and I knew that some day I should have to go through that door like a schoolteacher ushering in the kids and find me and Danny and his father and Isaac and his father, all there in a kind of book or something and I should have to explain the way in which Mr Pratt had died.

When I came back from the funeral Lancaster and Mr Brown and Mr Pinkofsky from the Royal were talking about making a film. They sat around our parlour table. Mr Pinkofsky had decided that the little sequence which had proved to be so popular at his cinema deserved to be extended. Therefore he had put up the money to make a film incorporating the process of vocalisation as he called it. He had decided that what the public really needed was a curious amalgam of both silence and speech. He had hit on the idea of making a silent film in the usual manner but whereas the traditional film would have showed captions indicating something of what had just been uttered by the actors the revolutionary film would be intercut with a vision of Mr Brown speaking the words.

When they had explained to me what they intended to do I said, 'Tha means like the Bellman.'

'What about Bellman?' Mr Brown sounded mystified.

'Oh, it's nowt,' I said. 'It's just that I used to imagine the Bellman as a kind of narrator in a play. I used to think that the actors were nowt but bits and pieces in the head of the story-teller. I think I had the idea that we were nowt but bits and pieces in Jacky Jellis's head, that's how he knew what was goin' on.'

121

'That's brilliant,' Lancaster said. 'We'll use the Bellman.'

Mr Brown was overjoyed – I think more at not having to appear in any more of Lancaster's experimental works rather than with my idea – but he twinkled at me nonetheless and he said, 'Tha's a genius, lad,' and I suddenly felt incredibly important.

The three film makers set about producing their talking picture with the help of Jacky Jellis. The Bellman was a most unlikely film star. Though the sun shone he insisted upon wearing his oilskin cape and fisherman's hat. He persisted too in sitting in the rubber chair to speak his lines and in holding the bell on his knee. Each of his short speeches was preceded by a loud ringing noise and it was only because of Lancaster that he didn't introduce each of his lines with the word *sithee*.

'It's sithee this and sithee that,' Lancaster told him, 'tha'll have to stop it, Jacky, or we'll get another for the part.'

The Bellman, who had seen Mr Brown's masterly performance in the first short sequence which was packing them in at the Royal, eyed our lodger with some concern and obviously decided there and then that he had better take direction from my uncle if he wasn't to lose his part to the most famous talking star of them all. But let me come back to the film later on – it's time now to close the nine days.

We are now into the final day of the General Strike, the signpost up at the crossroads is still turned so that the Leeds-bound traffic is directed into the village. H. G. Wells has taken off Marlene Jellis to God knows where, we've buried Danny Pratt's father and Marlene's father is about to star in the most important film ever in the history of the cinema. At about eleven o'clock that morning a pair of camels led by a couple of bedouin gentlemen appeared on the rise up by the big house and proceeded sure of foot down into the village. Behind them was a whole ordered zoo of other circus animals. There were horses and giraffes, vicuna and goats. There were lions and tigers locked in their cages, safely stowed on the backs of giant lorries which puffed smoke like loosed railway engines. There were dozens of caravans housing all of the circus performers who waved from behind the windows as the procession went by. Bringing up the rear were a dozen elephants. As the two bedouins approached one of them asked if this was the way to Leeds and Billy, with eyes as wide as those he would produce to greet a Martian, said, 'Ay. Keep straight on,' and the camels led off, drawing the circus up Hunger Hill.

We watched spellbound as the troupe went by and Billy asked me if I hadn't recognised Rosanne and Clarrie in one of the caravans. I shook my head – a youth who imagined insurance salesmen to be from Mars might see anything. Lancaster was filming everything and his lens followed the circus as it left us, negotiating the slope of Hunger Hill without too much difficulty. As the last elephant's bottom disappeared from view over the purple summit of the hill I knew that the strike was over. I knew that out there beyond Hunger Hill the strike was finished. The elephants would herald a new dawn for them o'er yonder. An elephant's bottom symbolised too the closing of an age in our village – a different age. It was a last bottom wedged in that trapdoor in the sky to the east of our village. In the morning it would blot out the rising sun.

Seeing the Bellman still sitting in the chair, I thought that perhaps he might have said that it was the end of the age of the open flower. I could sense the flower closing again. It had spat out its kids – Lancaster hadn't been one of them. The open flower had also taken in the outside world but not any more. A policeman would watch the crossroads from now on. That was the last procession. That elephant's rump was the rear-end view of the last visitor from an ancient time. There was electricity and wireless but they weren't quite the marvels that they had been. We were growing old, were Billy and I. As I told you, I was locked in the coal and nearly ready for the pit.

10

The rubber woman

After the departure of Marlene Jellis the schoolmaster became more morose. He could hardly manage to take himself off to school on a morning. He would sit at his little table, breakfasting on jam and bread and sucking the sweetness out of his tash with copious backwashings of tea. He always ate Mrs Gill's strawberry jam at breakfast time – it was sweeter than most, for Mrs Gill added the extra sugar which crystallised in his facial hair. And it was more red; Mrs Gill also added cochineal, a dye made from the squashed bodies of a silvery Mexican insect. It imparted the colour of the fresh wild fruit to her confection.

It was usually whilst he washed his plate and his chipped mug that Miss Fountaine would ring the school bell. He hoped that it would be Marlene ringing the bell but he knew that it never was. He could tell the difference between the noises the bell made when it was shaken by Marlene and by Miss Fountaine. The headmistress's ringing was tuneful, she taught the children to sing, you know, whereas the bell in Marlene's hands was less melodic – more of a clang than a ring. Despite his love for the woman, he knew her to be a dull ringer of bells. On the other hand she held the bell in such a manner that it excited him. He liked to watch Marlene holding the bell. After Miss Fountaine had called the children to school he would sit a while, trying to shake the images of Marlene from his grieving head and listen to the footsteps scurrying past his door.

On one such morning, whilst he was still eating his jam and bread and before the bell had been rung, there was a knock at his door. It startled him for a moment. There were very few knocks on Mr Piggott's door. Sometimes a mischievous child might bang on it as he went by, but Wenceslas would always hear the running steps fading quickly away on such occasions. He waited at his table and heard nothing more than the knocking. Then he waited some more and there was another knock.

'Who is it?' he called, without bothering to get up from the table.

'It's Lancaster Brightside, Mr Piggott. Does thee have a moment?'

The schoolteacher got up and let in my uncle. He was initially surprised to see that he was accompanied by a bald woman whom he'd not seen before, but failed to give the woman a second look before he took his depression back to the breakfast table.

'What is it, Lancaster?' he asked gloomily as he sat down.

'It's a rubber woman, Mr Piggott.'

'What?' said the schoolteacher. He still hadn't yet given of his time to cast the woman a second look.

'Ay. It were sent to me by Mr Tsiblitz. It's another of his inventions.'

'What's tha talkin' about, Lancaster?' Wenceslas asked with his head held in his hand and his elbow on the table.

'This, Mr Piggott. She's made of rubber.'

Mr Piggott looked more carefully at the person who had come through the door with my uncle. Besides being bald, she had the face of a young woman with perhaps a touch too much rouge, but wearing an older person's coat. In fact he thought it was the coat of Mrs Brightside, Lancaster's mother.

'Rubber?' he suddenly asked.

'Ay, she's not real. She's rubber, like the flying suits.'

The schoolteacher got up from his seat and touched the object about its face. He smiled. 'By, it's a good likeness, is that.'

'Ay, well it would be, if Mr Tsiblitz invented it. He sent it for me but my mother has told me to be rid of it.'

126

'Why?'

'Well, tha can hardly keep summat like this in the house, when there's all them others livin' there. Children and women and such.'

'What's tha talkin' about, Lancaster?' Mr Piggott asked again.

Lancaster looked embarrassed. 'Well, tha naws, tha can't go rumpin' and stuff with a house full of people.'

'Rumpin'?'

'Ay.'

Mr Piggott sat back into his chair and put his head in his hand again. Lancaster always had been a bit of a dream but the schoolteacher was now totally unable to comprehend what his former pupil was talking about.

'What's tha mean, rumpin', lad?' he asked slowly.

'Doin' it?' my uncle said. He couldn't be more specific than that and he pointed at the thing in his mother's coat.

'Doin' it with that?' Mr Piggott's voice rose an octave. He was not quite believing of the fact that he had asked the question.

'Ay.'

Lancaster undid the coat and let it drop from about the object's shoulders to reveal to the schoolmaster a body every bit as curved and creamy as that of Marlene Jellis. The breasts were full, the nipples large and pink; those of a young woman. The skin was white as milk and appeared to have a silken softness. There was a brush of pubic hair covering a thrusting mound, the belly was white and flat and the button like a vortex screwed his gaze into the model's femininity. Hair grew freely from the armpits just as it did from beneath Marlene's arms. Wenceslas was just beginning to contemplate the silken thighs when the bell rang. He knew instinctively that it was not the hand of Miss Fountaine for there was no music in the noise. Perhaps it was Marlene clasping the bell. Mr Piggott got an erection.

'Is thee all right?' my uncle asked, noting the painful and

127

awkward way in which the schoolteacher had risen up quickly from his seat.

'Well, what's tha want to bring it here for?' Mr Piggott asked, ignoring my uncle's concern, and, grabbing a book from his shelf, he limped out of the door.

When he had turned the corner and seen that it was not Marlene but Mr Clayton who was ringing the bell, the schoolmaster stopped in his tracks, but the caretaker had already spotted him approaching the school yard.

'Miss Fountaine's ill today,' he called out.

'Is Miss Jellis at school yet?' Mr Piggott called back.

'Not seen 'er.'

'Well, there's something which I have to do, Mr Clayton, so will tha put all the children together in one classroom and take the first lesson.'

'Me?'

'Yes, you, Mr Clayton. Tell the girls to get on with their sewing and read the boys a story or something.'

'Can't read, Mr Piggott,' the caretaker told him, removing his flat cap and scratching his bald head with his little finger and the one next to it; it was more a tickle than a scratch. Seeing the caretaker's hairless head reminded Wenceslas of where he must go and he quickly turned on his heels and headed back for his home just around the corner shouting angrily, 'Well, make one up, Mr Clayton, it's not that difficult.' He turned the corner in time to see Lancaster leaving the house. He lugged the object in his mother's coat after him.

'Lancaster, don't go,' he shouted. 'Don't leave just yet.'

My uncle turned and walked slowly back to Mr Piggott. 'Let's go back inside,' the schoolmaster said, anxious to usher him into the house again. 'Now, as I was askin' thee, why me, Lancaster?'

'Well, it'd be a shame to destroy it, Mr Piggott. But I got to thinking who might tek it and I thought, well, it would have to be a bachelor and one who lives alone at that.'

'But why, lad? I don't understand. Why a bachelor?'

'Like I told thee, Mr Piggott. Because of rumpin'.'

'Rumpin', Lancaster? Tha keeps telling me about the rumpin' but tha's not explaining thaself too well. What's tha mean?'

My uncle shuffled and then he said, 'Well, I thought with Marlene going off like that tha'd be lonely, Mr Piggott. I thought she might cheer thee up.' He patted the arm of the rubber woman. Then it suddenly occurred to Lancaster that perhaps Mr Piggott hadn't quite understood the function of the object which he had brought for him. 'It's not just a good likeness, Mr Piggott,' he said, 'it's more than that, it's got 'oles.'

''Oles?'

'Ay, 'oles. In the right places, Mr Piggott. There's 'oles.' Light then dawned on the face of the schoolteacher and he quickly undid the coat and gave the specimen a thorough investigation. When my uncle left, Mr Piggott's erection had returned.

The first thing which Wenceslas did was to buy his rubber woman a ginger wig. He let the hair hang loose and he tucked her up in his bed and let the hair flow over the silken milky white body and touch her bottom. Then after a couple of days he went to see Jacky Jellis and told him that Marlene had come home and that she was moving into his house with him and that she had sent him to get some of her clothes. Jacky gave him Marlene's dresses and her underclothes and stockings and he took some of her perfume and her jewellery too. Her father asked if he could come down to see Marlene but Wenceslas told him that she didn't want to see her father, not just yet, but that he would send her to see him as soon as she felt better about it. That really upset Jacky because his children had never stopped loving their father, they were always pleased to see him and he couldn't understand what had gotten into his daughter to make her not want to see her father.

Wenceslas took the clothes home with him and dressed up the rubber woman and had her sit with him in the parlour. He put her right by the window so that people could see in and note that Marlene was back and was living in the house of a man who wasn't her husband. Which of course wasn't untrue. He'd show them, her and that H. G. Wells. The clothes were slightly too big for the rubber woman so Wenceslas spent several days making alterations. He sat at his parlour table each morning before school started, cutting and sewing and stitching and eating his strawberry jam and drinking his tea. The tea would drip from his tash, and once or twice it dripped on to Marlene's dresses but he didn't care, he was too obsessed with his new toy to worry about tea stains on her clothing. He went into Leeds and bought a golden brooch like the one which she had always worn, the one which held her together, and he clipped it to her dress.

Then one day he did her hair up in a bun, dressed her in her altered clothes and took her for a spin in his car. He drove past our terrace and waved and we all commented how well Marlene looked after her time with the futurologist: even Lancaster was taken in by it all. Mr Clayton asked when Marlene would be going back to school and Wenceslas said that she wouldn't be going back because she was pregnant. That shocked Miss Fountaine and it shocked my grandmother too – despite the fact that my cousin Clarrie was illegitimate. Schoolteachers are different, she said, which was just what Wenceslas Piggott had wished her to say. He was making sure that if she ever truly came back, Marlene would never work at the school again.

He drove her about all over the place. The policeman at the crossroads saw them regularly and each time they passed Wenceslas would make certain that he was seen to be engrossed in conversation with his companion. He would lean towards her and sometimes nudge her, saying things like 'You women, you're all alike. Always going on about something or other.' Then the policeman would smile and think how those two were always going on at each other. Lovers' tiffs!

Whenever he bought his strawberry jam from Mrs Gill she would ask after Marlene and he would say that she was doing very well.

'Is she getting bigger?' Mrs Gill would ask.

'Oh ay. Much,' he would answer. 'Gettin' bigger every day. We think it might be twins.' And Mrs Gill would pass on the good news to my grandmother and soon everyone in the village would know how well Marlene was doing. It was the one thing which Jacky Jellis seemed not to know, for whenever he came to give us the news we would first of all have to give him ours.

'Tha Marlene's doing fine.' He had to know that first then he would ring his bell and get on with telling us what he knew.

One day Wenceslas took her up to the crossroads. Waiting to turn right on to the Wakefield road, he noticed the policeman sitting by the signpost eating his sandwiches and he said loudly, 'Look, dear, bobby's havin' 'is lunch,' but the policeman was too busy reading his newspaper to notice them. As he made the turn another car smashed right into them and there was a terrible explosion. The policeman, when he described it, said that it was just as if a bomb had gone off. The second motorist fainted and had to spend a week in the hospital. He was unable to remember anything about the crash and had a permanent tremor for the rest of his life. When the policeman ambled over to see what had happened, Wenceslas was already gathering together the pile of clothes from the front seat and was tucking them under his arm. The policeman asked the schoolteacher what had happened and Wenceslas, seeing that the other motorist was unconscious, blamed the poor fellow completely. He was unable to account for the explosion, he said, but he was sure that the report had originated in the other person's car. He left his own vehicle parked up by the crossroads and wandered down to the village with Marlene's clothes bundled in his arms.

'Is Marlene getting any bigger?' our neighbour asked as the schoolteacher passed.

'She's exploded, Mrs Gill,' he answered and, mildly concussed, he wandered on his way, arms filled with her voluminous clothing. Of course my grandmother soon got to know of this and eventually it came to the ears of the Bellman too. Jacky Jellis wasn't going to let it rest at that; he wanted to know what had happened to his daughter. He went round to see Wenceslas Piggott, together with my grandmother. At first the schoolmaster wasn't going to let them in but Jacky threatened him with the police and he finally opened the door.

'Where's my Marlene?' the Bellman asked.

'She ran off with Mr Wells.'

'Ay, but she cem back. Tha took her clothes, Wenceslas. Now where is she?'

'She's gone back to Mr Wells, I'm tellin' thee.'

'But tha's still got her clothes. No woman would go off without her clothes,' my grandmother told him.

'I haven't, I haven't got her clothes at all,' Wenceslas said.

'Don't lie. It only makes it worse. Mrs Gill saw thee with her clothes when tha came into the village t'other day. Now where is she, lad?' my grandmother persisted.

'I've told thee, she's gone off with H. G. Wells.'

'Right,' said Jacky, 'I'm going for bobbies,' and he went off and brought a policeman from the station at Castleford. The policeman searched through the house and found Marlene's clothes stuffed under Mr Piggott's bed. There was a nasty hole right through the dress just about where her heart would have been. And the hole was bang in the centre of a nasty red sticky patch which looked suspiciously like blood.

'No, it's not,' said Wenceslas when challenged. 'It's strawberry jam and tea which has dripped from my tash.'

But the policeman wouldn't hear of it and he arrested the schoolteacher. He took him off to the station and cautioned him, which prompted Mr Piggott to partially tell the truth. He told his interrogators that Marlene had met with an accident whilst in his car. He explained that was how there came to be a hole in the dress but the admission only got him into deeper trouble. The police could find no blood in the car. And of course neither the policeman at the crossroads nor the second motorist could remember seeing a woman in the car at the time of the accident.

'He just seemed to be keen to be off. And off with the lady's clothes which were on the front seat,' said the policeman, imparting a significance to the event which it didn't have.

When they had submitted the clothing to some tests, however, and found that the red stains were not bloodstains an even great confusion found its way into the case.

In the meantime the village children were without a schoolteacher, for Miss Fountaine, who had been nicely on her way to recovery, suffered a relapse of her illness when she heard that Mr Piggott had been arrested on suspicion of murdering Miss Jellis. Each day all the children went up to the crossroads to look for the clues which might lead to an explanation for Marlene's sudden disappearance. Then one day a small boy turned up a piece of something which when he handed it to Billy and me had us both quaking in our shoes. We were thirteen years old now and knew what it was immediately. It was a rubbery piece of skin with a hole in it and the whole thing was surmounted by a mass of curly hair.

'Is it what I think it is?' I asked.

'Cunt, daft.'

'By gow. He's cut her up into little bits,' I told him and he nodded gravely, then we solemnly went off to the police station in Castleford to show them our find.

The detectives were mystified as they stretched the

material this way and that. They turned it over and did the same, causing the occasional hair to fall out.

'What is it?' asked one of the detectives, handing it back to Billy.

'Don't tha want it?' he asked back.

'Not particularly. What is it?'

'Cunt,' Billy told him in a whisper.

'It's what?'

'Cunt,' I said as softly as I could manage. We were promptly ejected together with our evidence.

The case of the missing schoolteacher made the local papers. The police, puzzled by the lack of a body, began to suspect that Wenceslas might have got rid of Marlene by dissolving her in acid. An examination of his home however showed that there were no traces of either blood or acid, even in the drains. Suspicion then turned to burial as a means of disposal and the police began to look for freshly dug earth in and around the village. They found a recently dug patch by the Roman wall at the summit of Hunger Hill. The disturbed soil went down about as far as one might stick a corpse but there was no body. In fact there was nothing buried in the patch at all and that puzzled the police too. Then one day when Mr Brown overheard two policemen talking about the recently dug hole on Hunger Hill – he had been taken to the station on suspicion of having stolen more bags – he suddenly realised that it must have been the spot where Great Great Grandmother had hidden her loot. Nobody had buried anything on the hill, he said to my father, but Albert had certainly dug up something from there. Meanwhile all that Wenceslas Piggott would say was that Marlene had gone off with Mr Wells.

11

Archie Jellis, Bruno and Bottom Boat Beauty

During that period of his sister's disappearance and the detainment of Mr Piggott, Archie Jellis was in his final year at Charing Cross Medical School. He never wore the tie and could never have afforded to buy the blazer. He had a doctor's white coat and a stethoscope, both of which he had been able to purchase out of the ten pounds which his father had given him. He always borrowed the books he needed for his studies from the other students. They mostly thought him an odd ball and they didn't care for him very much. He was not of their kind. To pay his fees he picked up work in restaurants, washing dishes here and there. After midnight he would then take home the scrapings from the customers' returned plates and share his one meal a day with Bruno. Sometimes he was unable to find work and he and Bruno would have to resort to some other means of feeding themselves.

One day, at a time when he was unable to find work to support himself, he received a letter from his father and slipped it neatly folded into his pocket without opening it, thinking that he would read it whilst he had his meal. He had eaten in a different place on each of the last dozen nights. He left his cold flat, holding Bruno at the end of a bit of rope, to look for yet a different eating house. He took the dog up the Strand past all the swank restaurants, passing by Covent Garden where he had savoured the fare in most of the smaller places during the last few weeks and went further afield and into Holborn. There he found a pie shop. He tied Bruno's rope to the leg of the chair on which he sat and asked the dog to lie down. Bruno obediently curled at

Archie's feet and sniffed the cooking smells out of the warm air. A waiter dressed in a starched white apron came to his table and Archie ordered a large eel pie with mash and peas. He read his father's letter with tears in his eyes for he learned that his sister had disappeared and that Mr Piggott, the schoolteacher, had been arrested on suspicion of having murdered her. His father wanted him to go home for a while; until all this muddle has been sorted, he wrote. Bruno could see the emotional struggle which the letter had triggered in his master's head and he stared at Archie with big brown eyes. Then very suddenly tears flowed over his snout and on to the floor where he was lying. He didn't make a sound. He just let the tears flow silently, wetting the pale linoleum. Archie continued his meal in thoughtful silence. When he had eaten a little more than half of his dinner he called the waiter to his table and asked him if he would put the rest of the food into a bag so that he could take it home for his dog. The waiter took the food back to the kitchen and returned a minute later with the remainder of the meal neatly packaged up. Archie slipped the packet into his jacket pocket – he still wore his Sunday best – and asked the waiter if he could direct him to a toilet. The man showed him out through the tiny kitchen to a red brick toilet in the yard at the back of the shop. When the waiter had returned to the kitchen Archie heaved himself over a wall and ran off.

Naturally the waiter assumed that Archie would be returning even when it was apparent that he was no longer in the toilet – after all, he had left his dog who lay down in a small pool of tears and was still tethered to the chair. It is curious that the waiter in the starched apron should not have assumed the wet to be something other, but he knew it to be a puddle of tears thus he never scolded the dog. He just patted him and said, 'There, there. Has your master gone and left you? It's a shame. Isn't it a shame? He'll be back, I expect, just you wait and see. There there.' Then he went off to the kitchen to bake more pies.

Bruno patiently waited for Archie to return. Bruno was a good actor and he knew exactly what he had to do. He waited. As only a dog can wait, he waited. Then at about midnight with the moon up and bright in the sky, Bruno was kicked out with a curse and sent off to stray about the Inns of Court. But Bruno knew his way home from almost anywhere in London. Back at the cold flat he received his share of the meal, barked softly at the moon and the stars and then curled up with Archie he fell into a deep slumber.

In his time as a schoolteacher, Wenceslas Piggott had three pupils of whom he could be justly proud – four if you count Marlene, but I think that Wenceslas stopped counting Marlene when all this muddle was over.

There was my uncle Lancaster, the famous film maker and aerial photographer. There was myself, the literary prize winner and curator of the strange museum – I didn't tell you about that yet. Then there was Archie Jellis who after qualifying as a doctor went on to become the president of the Royal College of Physicians, a man with rooms in Harley Street. Of the three it was Archie of whom Mr Piggott would have been the most proud. Archie's achievement was nothing short of a miracle. He had got the brains, that was never in dispute. But his ability to overcome adversity, to take on the establishment and play them at their own game and to win – to win right through to the very pinnacle of his profession – that was Archie's achievement. And for Mr Piggott it was a miracle. It was the miracle which he would have liked to have quoted to succeeding generations of pupils had he been allowed – take heart, he would have said, look at the miracle of Archie Jellis, old boy of this school.

You see, Lancaster never had to overcome adversity. In his early years he had the backing of my great great grandmother's fortune; she got him started. Then Mr Tsiblitz had moulded the fear out of him – as a boy he had overcome his

137

fear of flying. And Pinkofsky too – he had provided encouragement and finance in the early years. Brains were something with which my uncle was never blessed, nor, as it turned out, did he need them.

As for me, like I have said elsewhere, I just fell from my mother's womb spouting water and words – neither of which has much to do with being brainy. A parrot in the rain can manage the same. The museum was a mixture of luck and acquisition, the latter a notion learned from Mr Brown and a paper bag. No, Lancaster's mastery of his craft and my eventual rise to success had nothing whatsoever to do with the miraculous. Archie, though, Archie was a miracle.

The first that I knew of Archie's return was when, looking from the window, I saw Bruno wandering into the yellow laboratory and sniffing at my duck. I left the house and said, 'Hello, Bruno. Did they teach thee to be human down in London?' The old dog just stared at me with his intelligent eyes and all of those old feelings started to flow back into my head. 'I don't know, Bruno,' I told him. 'I don't know why it's like that, but we must be thankful for what we are and that we're alive, that's what my grandmother says and I think she must be right. So stop looking at me that way, will thee? Why don't thee just go off and behave like other dogs?'

I watched Bruno sneak off with his tail between his legs and as he left the laboratory Archie appeared at the entrance.

'Hello, young 'un,' he said. 'How are you getting on?'

'I'm alreet, Archie. Is tha doctoring now?'

'Not yet. Not properly. I'll soon be qualified though.' He smiled at me.

I picked up my duck and threw him into his rain barrel. He promptly turned himself upside down and we both watched him floating about like that.

'Can I ask thee summat?'

'What is it, Donald? What do you want to know?'

'What's tha Bruno been up to?'

'Oh, his usual tricks, you know. He likes it in London.'

'No, Archie. I mean, will tha tell me how come Bruno saw thee through tha studying?'

'Well, he just looked after me like he always did.'

'Tha father told us tha wouldn't starve, not with Bruno. Did tha beg in t'streets or do a turn or summat?'

'Oh, that. Well, we sort of did a turn and it was a kind of begging I suppose.' Archie then told me the story of how when he had no money he would take Bruno to a restaurant and tie him to a chair. He told me the whole tale of how he managed to eat and get food for the dog too.

When he had finished I said, 'That's not begging, that's thieving. Tha means tha's a thief, Archie.'

'No, Donald. I'm a student doctor.'

'Ay, well, tha's a thief as well, then.'

'Let's say that I could never have become a doctor, if I hadn't learned a bit of thieving first, then.'

'Ay, alreet, we'll say that then.'

Archie wandered off, whistling for his dog. I saw Bruno come hurtling past me, chasing after his master with feathers falling from his jaws, and I ran as quickly as I could to the laboratory. There were a few brown feathers floating on the skin of water. There were feathers on the grass close by the rain barrel. I ran back on to the common.

'Tha bastard, Bruno,' I shouted after the disappearing figures. 'Tha's eaten up my fuckin' duck.' I watched them now very small walking away from me. I was crying my heart out and the world was changing about me. I had no idea how to prevent it from changing.

When Mr Piggott saw Archie at the police station in Castleford he burst into tears too.

'Where's my sister, Mr Piggott?' Archie asked gently.

'She's with Mr Wells, Archie. I swear to God, she's with Mr Wells.'

'That'll do for me, Mr Piggott, but nobody else seems to believe you. Did anyone try contacting Mr Wells to see if your story was true?'

'I don't know, Archie. Thank God tha's here, lad, thank God.' Then the schoolteacher broke down, warbling great incoherent sobs. Archie waited for the man to cry himself out. Then in the relative calm which followed he asked Wenceslas Piggott to tell him all about it. Archie listened patiently as the schoolteacher spoke. At last, a real doctor had come to our village, even if he was a thief.

'I fell in love with a rubber doll, Archie. I dressed her up in Marlene's clothing. I just wanted to show 'em. Show all the villagers and Marlene and Mr Wells. I wanted to show 'em that I could be just as good as them. Have my respect. I wanted to show 'em all, so I dressed the doll in Marlene's clothes. I took her to my bed at night and I took her out in the car during the day and told 'em she was pregnant. She was beautiful, Archie, every bit as lovely as tha sister. Then when the bloody thing exploded I didn't know what to do. I couldn't tell anyone, not really, because I had their respect now and I wasn't going to lose it, Archie. I'm not going to lose that respect now. But nobody's hurt. There was no murder or owt like that, it was a doll, Archie, a bloody doll and I loved her. Marlene went off with Mr Wells, I swear to God she did and she's not been back.'

Archie went back down to London and found his sister living with Mr Wells under the assumed name of Sosthenes Smith and he took her to the police station and had her identify herself. Archie was never short of money after that. His sister and Mr Wells always saw that he was properly housed and fed until he had qualified in medicine. After finding his sister he came back to the village immediately and took Doctor Cartwright down to the police station with him and he asked Mr Piggott to repeat his story to the doctor. The schoolteacher told his story again, explaining

140

his love for a rubber doll which had long since exploded, and they both certified him and had him put in Wakefield asylum.

When all this muddle was over and Archie was about to go down to London to finish his studying he came round to our house with Bruno.

'I'll be living with my sister from now on,' he told us, 'so I'll not be having any need of the dog. I thought Donald might like to have him. He's not got much time left and I think he would be happy to finish his old days with your Donald.'

'Bruno, why'd th'eat my duck?' was the very first thing that I asked him when Archie had gone. He stared at the sky. Then he barked and the sky began to rain great drops; as blue as distant hills.

I never let him forget that he had eaten the duck. Sometimes he would climb into the rain barrel and just sit. He couldn't help it – Doctor Cartwright said that it was obsessive behaviour but it was odd to see a black dog half submerged in the rain-water like that. Sometimes when the barrel was a bit more full he would duck his head for a few moments, then lift it out and shake off the water with a few strong shakes of his ears and he would fling the water in the pattern of stars in a spiralling galaxy sometimes as far as the window. My father, sitting in a wide winged chair and reading his newspaper beneath the electric light, would lift his head and ask, 'Hello, is it raining again?'

Bruno died the following year and I buried him in the laboratory and inscribed his name on one of the yellow stones. 'Bruno and duck,' it read, 'who died with all the sadness of knowing exactly who he was and of who he might have been.'

The coal owners mourned the passing of our country's greatness. Britain wasn't paying her way in the world, which to them was another way of saying that we were not exporting a sufficient quantity of coal. World markets were expanding and we were selling less, that was why we had so much unemployment – that's what they told us. Then they told us that the only way to reduce unemployment was to export more coal. To export more coal they would have to reduce the selling price and the reduction in price was dependent on the miners accepting a cut in wages.

Of course this kind of logic didn't just apply to coal, it applied to everything. We had to pay our way in the world. Nobody seemed to be asking why the government didn't stimulate demand at home. Nobody seemed to be advocating higher wages and making things for home consumption to take up the extra spending power. Mr Piggott, he once mentioned it. He told my grandmother that there should be factories all over the country churning out pot ducks for the walls in people's parlours and that the coal owners should be giving each collier an extra sixpence per shift so that they could buy them. That would provide employment and step up the demand for more coal, he said. He was the only one I ever heard mention such a thing and look where he ended up. No, the conventional wisdom was that we should accept less pay to make the country great again and the amazing thing is that we did.

It was also amazing that we survived the strikes and lock-outs of 1926. We were paid benefit by the union but by July the fund was exhausted. Then other trade unions sent donations and there were many fund-raising activities organised by the church and by local people. But Emily wouldn't have that – despite the fact that we were all in the same boat and self-respect had given way to a communal concern for survival. My grandmother was made of a different material to the others. Her pride was her pride and she needn't follow the sheep. It confounded us all and had us thinking of other means by which we could be supported.

Mr Henderson had a greyhound. She was a cross-eyed brindle bitch who slept in one of his armchairs and she could run like the wind, especially if he had lathered her backside with turpentine. Her name was Bottom Boat Beauty but she was anything but beautiful. Mr Brown preferred to call her Bottom Boat Wonder because with those cross eyes, he said, when she raced it was a wonder that she could see the hare at all. She snoozed all day in her armchair and rarely took exercise but Mr Henderson used to take her all over Yorkshire and have her race against other pitmen's greyhounds. Bottom Boat Beauty rarely lost a race. Now Mr Brown saw in this squint-eyed, lazy good-for-nothing a way of making money. Not in backing her to win – the odds were far too short even if you could find someone to accept your bet – but in backing her to lose. To effect such a phenomenon he had to bring Bottom Boat Beauty together with yet another marvel of technology – a wonder of an ancient technology. My grandmother's dumplings. Emily Brightside's dumplings were in their way just as famous as the brindle bitch. Ernest maintained that a dozen were sufficient to sink a battleship. And Mr Brown thought quite rightly that three or four would be enough to sink Bottom Boat Beauty.

Twice a week he would go to some far-flung pit village together with old man Henderson. The racing bitch had already been weighted with my grandmother's dumplings and trotted lithely along at the end of a stout rope. The wily villagers, remembering the pasting which had been meted out to their local champion only a short while before, would put all of their available cash on the visiting dog whilst Mr Brown would back the recently defeated local. He always got good odds and usually managed to clean up. Then the three of them would return triumphant to our village, the brindle bitch still springy of step and trotting along between the two smiling men. Mr Brown would then divide the winnings between the two households. My grandmother, although she never approved of gambling, accepted that in the special circumstances it was a legitimate source of income and a good deal better than falling back on charity. She never knew why Mr Brown was so keen on her dumplings but was flattered that he should eat so many of them and her pride was maintained.

12

'Grandmother, Grandmother, come and see'

The project which saved the whole village from starvation in the latter period of the strike, though, was Lancaster's talking picture. The film was finished late in August and had an immediate showing at the Royal Picture Palace. Lancaster received a commission of a penny a seat from Mr Pinkofsky – a penny per arse as the proprietor put it – and it brought about five pounds a day into the village. That was just about enough to feed everyone. The film showing opened on a bright gusty day when the local farmers were sheaving the crop and we walked in twos from the village, like they did when Mr Piggott had the smaller children out for a nature ramble. Filled with gossip we trudged across fields and counted the twisted trees which grew from the coal-cut land. Those who had trained their ears to recognise a pitman's tappings in the earth had no difficulty in hearing the slugs slurp at the ripe corn. The wind's bluster tossed black dust from our village into the warm air and birds fell among it, blotting out the sun. I saw Isaac racing through a hail of sparrows, whirling his wooden clapper at them and causing the storm to take back to the skies as suddenly as it had arrived and miraculously the birds lifted the coal dust with them. For a time it was dark in heaven whilst below in the bright stage-set world Isaac's mother thonged a yellowed sheaf. I waved and Isaac waved back but we didn't speak.

We took a short cut through Mouldy Orchard where the plums were ripe and falling from the trees. The blackberries were large and several people stopped to pick them and when we came from the Orchard and entered Aken Jugs those who had taken the berries all had blue tongues and lips. There were earwigs carried on the wind and every so often somebody would fall out of line to brush them from their hair or from the hair of their companions. It was that kind of gusty day.

It has been said of the motion picture industry that its problem was that it could talk before it could think. Well, my sister Irene Rose went one better: as you know, she could talk before she was born. Lancaster's film opened with a grey shot of my sister. She was sitting on the grass on the common outside our house. She had on a dress which I think used to be my own and she showed the dimples in her chubby knees and thighs, pumping her elbows excitedly. These were the bellows which fanned the flames of our enthusiasm; we were alive to the picture maker's illusions. It was a picture of an ordinary babe with fair hair who wore a quizzical expression. You could see the smoke curling from the chimney behind her. It wound into a cheerless sky, curling and questioning. Irene Rose was talking. Mouthing baby words to the silent camera before her.

The scene faded to a flickering dark. There were white spots flashing on and off the screen. An image was trying to find its way to the hushed audience. The whirring noise of the projector, even though it was in a separate room, was getting into the auditorium. We held our breath, trying to make out the voice above the whirring projector. The image on the screen was still trying to put itself together – then suddenly the Bellman appeared; he looked like the man on the matchbox. Then it dawned on me. Jacky Jellis was the man on the matchbox. Jacky Jellis was the pilot, guiding us on a ship so vast that we couldn't see the sides. He was sitting in the rubber chair. He held the bell like the pilot grabs the wheel, then he shook the bell and whilst we still held our breath we could faintly discern the bell's ringing. We stared at his whiskery lips and saw him say in the same squeaky voice as that of Mr Brown on the first film, 'Granmovver, Granmovver, come an' see. There's unter Lancaster with a camera.' The image of the Bellman held and then he said, 'There's a whole world out there, Granmovver,' and I thought, that's odd, because I hadn't thought that Irene Rose had said anything of the sort. The Bellman continued with his monologue. 'Come an' see. Come an' see,' he seemed to be saying over and over again in a thin squeaky voice. The audience was spellbound. The shot of the Bellman slowly faded and another image formed on the screen. We watched the circus passing through the village and climbing Hunger Hill. There were the camels led by the two bedouins and the goats and the lions and all the rest. Then as the caravans passed and one took account of all those frozen faces, I distinctly saw Rosanne and Clarrie smiling from a small window and I thought, Billy, Billy – tha's got it right, Billy. Why did I ever doubt thee? Willmott is a Martian after all – a Martian and an earthling. There is no difference between Mars and Earth. They're interchangeable.

The Bellman was still talking, talking over the pictures. 'It's a fantastic world, if you will only give it a chance to come to you. Look at that elephant, look at the way its bottom moves as it climbs into the sky. Look at the way it starts to fill the door in the sky up there.' The scene slowly faded with the elephant's bottom wedged at the top of Hunger Hill exactly as I had remembered it and filling up most of the screen and I thought, Jacky, how's tha know these things? How's tha know what we're thinking? 'Don't let it go from you. You have to know when to hold. When to drop anchor and say this must be the place. Yes, look, I recognise it – even though it's only a patch of sea in an even greater ocean – you have to be able to recognise it.' The audience was gripped by a view of the water in the rain barrel outside our house. There was no duck, no movement. Just Jacky talking over the image of the still water. 'Let it come, let it come and see it for what it is,' the Bellman's voice said.

'That's right,' I said to myself. 'I'll not let it go. That's why I remember it like I do. Like the camera does too. It's stuck there, in that hole in the sky and it'll not go.'

The hushed audience were hypnotised by the succession of images. People whom they all knew appeared one at a time. They were persons who, if on some other occasion the audience had seen them on film, they might have laughed at, they might even have jeered at.

Charlie Gill stood in his doorway with his arm about his mother. He stood quite still, balanced on his one leg, and he smiled for the camera. Mr Doyle appeared in his piggery and he slapped a pig on the rump with his one big hand and the pig ran off and we had to imagine the squealing because Jacky was saying, 'Faces, faces,' over and over again and the portraits lingered in their sombre tones – one after the other – like the sepia images which ran in Lancaster's head. Then there was film of Mr Pinkofsky sitting in my aunt Henrietta's striped deckchair in the laboratory. He has a neat tash and his hair parted in the middle and greased back with cream. He looks just like my grandfather. Mr Pinkofsky smiles and nods at the camera, then by means of some cinematographic deception we see that it isn't Mr Pinkofsky at all, but my grandfather himself who smiles from the deckchair. Mr Brown appeared in his Sunday suit and everybody thought that he was going to say that stuff about God, but he didn't – he linked his arm into that of my mother and they both walked off on the common and the camera lingered after their back view as they went away like two people at the tail end of an old book. Then the scenes faded again and the Bellman was trying to form himself from out of the dark and finally he was there in the chair again and he said, 'Friends. And now, old friends,' and he faded again.

Now we saw film of the flying animals. Lancaster had edited in bits from some of his early experimental films, the ones he had made from a time before he had gone off to the War. You could sense a kind of fear in the audience. On the

148

one and only previous occasion when the flying animal sequence had been shown to the public – it had been an accident – the audience had greeted it rather coldly. They had believed it to be trick photography but it hadn't excited them. This audience was not as cynical – they believed in what they saw and their belief filled them with a kind of dread. 'Don't be afraid,' the Bellman said, anticipating their reaction. 'This also is a part of the coming world. Open up your hearts and let it be. You will be surprised at the wonders that will come. Grandmother, Grandmother, grab your spectacles – those which you share will do – and come and see.'

There's Mrs Henderson; she's dead now. And Charlie is there with his two legs. There's Albert – and he's gone – and William who now has children. There's Bill Pettit who was blown away at the Somme and Oliver who had a similar fate and look, there's Rosanne falling from her rope and Albert catching her, or was she catching Albert? Can you see Clarrie in her belly? Is the daughter in Albert's eye? Look. *Albert's dead in Bresci's hat.* I look about. Who said that? Was it merely whirring of the projector or was it yet another disembodied voice?

'Time's passing,' the Bellman told the silent audience. You could have heard a pin drop. 'Time, that's what it's all about. Follow that road, stay on it. It's all there is for you, but stay on the road. Fight for what's right – but don't get greedy or too curious, don't wander. Wandering's what'll get you in the end. So stay on the road and recognise when to drop anchor.'

The screen was now showing bits of film which Lancaster had taken here and there since he had returned from the War. Emily in the church at his brother's funeral. 'That's the grim funny business, that is, that wandering, that's the grim funny business,' Jacky said and I felt my grandmother shuffling on her orange box as she sat next to me in the quietened cinema. Then came an image of Lullaby Danny Pratt's father lying in a field. *Lancaster, how could you? How*

149

could you have filmed the poor man dead like that? Then the shocked audience gasps as the corpse struggles upright, whirling in the grey-filmed sequence, arms circling pell-mell, and the drunken man shambles off like a broken windmill. It wasn't *that* morning, the audience realises, and there is a huge sigh of relief breathed into the hot air of the cinema. Lancaster had just spotted him on any old morning. It had been Lullaby Danny Pratt's father drunk in the black and white fields like it always was – there was no blood, no red day.

There was film of the stars and of the moon which we could hardly tell from the blank and flickering screen which we received between sequences. There was film of Bruno barking at the sky and of Mr Brown blowing into a paper bag – only he seemed to be breathing from it. Lancaster had set up a reversal of reality and Mr Brown was taking from the bag as if it contained life-giving oxygen and one wanted almost to shout, don't take tha lips away, Mr Brown, don't present thaself to the rarefied atmosphere of the moon. I could hear Mr Brown wheezing away at the other side of my grandmother and the Bellman's squeaky voice was saying, 'Come and see the wonders of science. There's time. Don't be afraid. There's time because that is all there is. Do you understand? Do you see?' And as the voice finished its speaking the photograph of my great great grandmother was held on the screen. The photograph which Albert had taken of the old woman with Bresci's hat on her head and hugging the suitcase to her. Then she slowly faded away and the lights came up.

For about a full minute the audience stayed wrapped in a silence of their own thought. They were truly spellbound. Gradually they began to stir like dazed insects shaking off the effects of a freezing night. Then there was a sudden great clapping of hands. The volume was enough to hurt the ears as the applause turned to cheers and there were great stampings on the wooden floor. The Bellman was brought to the front of the cinema and asked to take a bow.

The farrier next door, who had been told to remain silent throughout the performance, brayed on his metal. Lancaster was brought forward and he too took a bow. Mr Pinkofsky stood between the star and the film maker and the three of them were cheered for a full half an hour until everyone was so tired and hoarse that they could neither shout nor clap nor stamp any more. So they just filed up from the upturned orange boxes and they touched the three of them in a loving kind of way as if they were just-born babies or something.

The film ran for months and people came from all over the country, and even from abroad, to see Lancaster's talking picture. Then one day Mr Pinkofsky said that we needed to transfer to a larger cinema because so many people wanted still to see the creation. And he said that if we were to show the film in another place it might as well be somewhere in which there was a decent amplification system. He looked about for the right theatre or hall but soon realised that the only places suitable were in London and nobody wanted to transfer the showing of the film down to London. Lancaster said that it wasn't because people down there didn't want to see the film, because they most certainly did, but he said that if it was shown in London nobody would understand it. He said that the only way in which the people from the south could understand was for them to come up and see the film in the coalfields. They should have to suffer the glitter of a diamond-hard night and listen to the squeaking of the wheel to understand what was in his film and you didn't get that sort of thing in London. Then Mr Brown suggested that we build a cinema in the village. One to house a thousand people and to have the best sound system in the world, and he asked Mr Pinkofsky if he could raise the money for such a venture. The proprietor imagined that there would be no difficulty in getting hold of the capital needed but after discussions with Joseph

151

Thwaite he learned that the coal owner was demanding a rent equivalent to fifty per cent of the audience receipts. After all, the village belonged to Thwaite, he told us – Mr Brown then remembered my birthright.

13

*Coming in on the wings of socialism, going out
touched by the world*

Some of you might know about my birthright; I wrote of it
in another place. Didn't I already tell you that when I was
born my maternal great grandfather, old man Thwaite,
came to see me? Didn't I tell you that? That was the time
when he cried on my mother's shoulder and called my
father Willie. Well, on that occasion he brought some
papers with him and he signed them with my great aunt
Henrietta's pen which was kept on the mantelshelf and he
gave the papers to my mother. This was my birthright – it
was the title deeds to the old disused pit and a little of the
land surrounding it at the bottom of Hunger Hill. The
disused pit is the one in which my great grandfather, James
Brightside, is buried; the one in which he found the dinosaur and in which he's buried because the bones tumbled
down on top of him.

It was common knowledge that I was the owner of this bit
of land. It hardly made me a capitalist – a clapped-out pit
filled with foul water and a pile of dinosaur bones – but
whilst the rest of us were discussing where best to locate
the proposed new cinema it was Mr Brown who remembered the birthright. That was the genius of Mr Brown; he
always could be relied on to find a solution to our problems.
They were never long-term solutions, but they directed us
away from the immediate crisis and if it was straight into
another one, well, that didn't matter. Mr Brown could
always find a way out of that one, too. He always saw the
simple way through the webs which we wove about ourselves. He was a guide, I suppose, taking us from one
marvellous bit of the woods to the next but never wholly

outside them – never beyond the trees – that was dangerous and he respected our rights to see the world only a bit at
a time.

'Of course,' said my father after Mr Brown had told him
that we could build on my land and that there would be
absolutely nothing that Joseph Thwaite could do about it.
'Why didn't I think of that?' That was the genius of Mr
Brown. He could always make people say those very
words.

Wagons brought the wood in the snow and the carpen-
ters from the pit knocked up the shell in a week. Thwaite
came down to make sure that we weren't using his nails
and his tools to execute the job. He had three inches of
snow on top of his hat. Pinkofsky had been extra careful
about his sourcing of materials and had bought everything
needed from reputable suppliers in Leeds. It was all ite-
mised on the invoices and the cinema owner took great
pleasure in showing them to my grandfather. Everything
down to the last tack had been paid for. Thwaite trudged
back up the hill, slipping in his galoshes as he climbed and
with an extra inch of snow on his hat.

Then they brought the bricks and everyone got on with
the building under the direction of Charlie Gill, who because he had only the one leg didn't seem to suffer from the
cold like everyone else. He said that having only one foot in
contact with the freezing ground made him only half as
cold as the rest of us. He was planted like a scarecrow in the
middle of the shell after they had put a floor down and he
shouted his directions all about as the four walls were
erected simultaneously.

They brought slates from Wales and tarpaulin from Dor-
set and they made pitch which smelled like cough drops
right there in great vats and the roofers got to work and had
a top on the building by the following week. Then the
electricians came in and fixed the sound system which had
come from America. It was called Movietone and in
America it told you the news – it was a sort of American

154

version of Jacky Jellis, I suppose. A bit flash compared with the Bellman but unlike Jacky it never knew what you were thinking. Whilst the electricians worked on the sound the carpets came and then the swank seating. There were no orange boxes now; only the best crushed velvet chairs. Rows and rows of them.

Before the strike ended the council sent some workmen to add a fourth arm to the signpost at the crossroads. The white finger pointed down the hill to New Royal Cinema – our village apparently still didn't warrant a name. Every evening hundreds of cars honked their way to the disused pit and Billy o' the Terrus End, wearing a peaked hat, directed the motorists to park in orderly fashion, in neat rows one behind the other. They were real nobs from London and places like that who had come to see the wonderful talking picture which like the village didn't even have a name. But the nobs weren't disappointed – they were processed with the courtesy they might have expected. Billy passed them on to Charlie Gill who wore a red commissionaire's uniform which displayed a dozen shining medals across his massive chest. He leaned on a crutch outside the cinema doors and all that brass and silver on his chest rattled as he hopped about directing the customers to the ticket office where his ancient mother dispensed tickets. Whilst the world gawped at the giant screen Billy and I would sit in one of the splendid motors lined up in the stillness of the car-park and listen to the voice of Jacky Jellis booming into the night through the windowless walls. Across at the terrace we could see our fathers and our neighbours sitting in their chairs and reading in parlours full of electric light. They were like wax figures at a sideshow. Beads of sweat stood out on their foreheads and one could only hope that the electric wasn't about to melt them down. Above us the canvas roof of the motor held back the moon and the falling stars and before long we knew Jacky's script by heart and could talk along with the Bellman. 'Grandmother, Grandmother, come and see.' We would always stop our conversation at that point. No matter what we were discussing, no matter how important it might have been, we stopped and waited and all three of us, Jacky, Billy and I, would shout into the night, 'Grandmother, Grandmother, grab your spectacles and come and see.'

Then as the performance closed to rapturous applause, Billy and I would scoot from the motor in which we happened to be sitting and the nobs would suddenly appear all at the same time and climb into their motors. But there was no orderly way of leaving, not like there had been an orderly way of arrival. Mr Brown said that they were only mirroring the way it was in life. He said that we came into this world in sequence – that we all had a number – but that the scramble out wasn't like that at all. It should have been but it wasn't. Apparently people, after they were born, couldn't be bothered to queue. We came in, ordered and socialist, but went out something else. Consequently we exited in a terrible mêlée, he told me. Billy and I would watch the motorists every night going forward, going back, unable to wait their turns, bumping and scratching, shouting dreadful obscenities at one another just like colliers in the drunken pub. Where's the difference? Billy asked. The nobs and the colliers – where's the difference? Every night we were treated to this messy exit from the village and every morning we would have a team of panel beaters bashing out the bumps in the bodywork and demanding payment from the owners who had been unable to leave and who had stayed the night in one of Rube Hardwick's done-up rooms above the pub.

It was because he had so many visitors that Rube needed the salmon. My father knew of a secret river tucked away in a green dale. It was a place where he took the blind and the daft in the Jam Sahib's motor. He had taken the blind and the daft up there for as long as I could remember – ever since my great great grandmother had bought the motor from Elyahou Tsiblitz. It was a secret place and because he only ever took the blind and the daft up there, it remained that way. When he heard of Rube's need he drove out alone one foggy morning and arrived back that same evening with sixty pounds of silver salmon piled on the back seat of the car. He charged Rube three shillings a pound plus his petrol money and an industry was suddenly born in our village. The second Mrs Doyle was a French chef of some distinction and turned out *darne de saumon du gave grillée au beurre blanc béarnaise* and *aiguillettes de saumon Turenne* and even *escalopes de saumon à l'oseille*. The food went down a treat at the pub and those who ate it always insisted on complimenting the chef, so at the end of the evening Rube Hardwick would produce Mrs Doyle from the kitchen and the lady would give a coy little curtsey and scurry back across the common to her husband where they would then feed the pigs with the fish heads and unpeg the condom from the washing line.

It was because Mr Doyle's piggery began to smell of fish that his neighbours complained. There was the permanent smell of fish in the air which when mixed with the natural smell of pigs produces something all the more disgusting for the olfactory lobes to cope with. He didn't do anything about it though – not until we all stopped buying his bacon because that had a fishy smell too. Then, of course, Mrs Doyle had a load of spare fish heads on her hands but my grandmother, suddenly aware of boundless opportunities, bought them from her for a penny each and produced masses of fish head pie which was just as legendary as her dumplings. At first, Rube Hardwick wasn't so very keen on offering it on his menu but was eventually persuaded to give it a try. The result was amazing. Not only did Rube now have to feed those who must spend the night waiting for the repair of their motors, but suddenly the cinema-goers were including a visit to the pub in their itinerary merely to sample the local fare before leaving the village. He served it like fish and chips, wrapped in newspaper. The nobs would take it back and eat it with their fingers in their motors or quite often they would stroll about the village staring in at the wax-like figures who read their newspapers in yellow rooms and deposit their own grubby newspapers outside our front doors for our mothers to sweep away in the mornings. My father tutted that the nobs had no manners.

For a time fish head pie became the most popular dish even among theatre-goers in the metropolis. Fish head pie restaurants sprang up in the West End of London and one or two of the more discerning proprietors paid my grandmother handsomely for her recipe and featured the authentic preparation on their menus – à la Emily Brightside. The second Mrs Doyle wasn't pleased. My grandmother was stealing her thunder and a great row was brewing. Mrs Doyle refused to sell her the fish heads any longer. A silly thing not to do, as my father was the one who controlled the supply, anyway. He simply lopped off the head and the tail of the salmon before he sold them to Rube and from then on the main ingredient didn't cost my grandmother anything at all. We were all learning the rudiments of capitalism and it was a relief to many when a halt was called to the strike and we could all go back to the mucky pit and forget our schemes for making ends meet.

All except me, that is. I had no wish to go into the pit. When we knew of the capitulation and that the strike had ended my father said, 'Time for the pit, Donald, tha'd better go and see deputy.' That's all he said to me. I shouldn't have expected more but I had kept alive a tired hope that he would ask me if there might be something else I would like to do with my life. He might have said, how about farming like Isaac's father or keeping pigs like Mr Doyle? What about the cinema like my uncle or doctoring like Archie Jellis? School-teaching, Simmonds' dye works, Gaylord's knicker factory, the church, the pub, the shops? Motor mechanic or water engineer? What about the police force or working at the gas works? But he didn't say any of that. Time for the pit, Donald. Time for the pit, son.

The deputy is a man in a strange position. He talks to everyone. He talks with the coal owner and with the manager and with the colliers, but nobody talks to him. Not unless they want something, then they talk with him. I needed something, or so my father told me. I needed to work in his stinking pit. So I had to go and see him.

His name was George Smart and he had a nose like a half-open knife blade. He was captain of the football team but after a game he would never take a drink at the pub with his team mates. Instead he would always go off and have a drink with the opposing side. Win or lose, it made no difference. He took his drink with the opposition. It wasn't that he didn't like the men in his team, it was just that he suffered the penalty of being deputy. That was the fate of a deputy. You drank with the opposition because none of your own would sup with you.

Of a morning, George Smart gave you eighty yards in which to discuss what you had to say. Take it or leave it. He lived in a neat cottage up by the big house and if you got out early enough you would stand outside George Smart's door and wait for him to begin his walk to the pit. If you were second in line, you stood by the way eighty yards from George Smart's door and on the path that you knew he would follow to work. If you were third in line, you stood a further eighty yards down the road. If you got as far as the pit and still had not found a place in the queue you had to wait until the following day before you could discuss matters with Mr Smart and you made sure that you got out early. Some people queued all night for Mr Smart. He called it the eighty-yard rule; others called it the eight-hour wait. He was a man of few words which was just as well, other-wise eighty yards would probably have been quite insufficient in which to settle matters.

'What's up, lad?' he said to me as the previous intervie-wee fell by the wayside.

'Start in t'pit, Mr Smart.'

'Name?'

'Tha knows me, Mr Smart. I sometimes come to training sessions for the football.'

'Name, lad?'

'Donald Brightside, Mr Smart.'

'Start tonight, lad.'

'But can't I start dayshift, Mr Smart? Go down with my father?'

'Start tonight, lad.'

'Yessir.'

'Report at pit head, we'll have thee sorted.'

'Right, Mr Smart.'

I fell back and saw Billy o' the Terrus End take my place a little further down the road.

14

Events leading to the foundation of the museum

On the nights which follow the bright red days, with the coal dust particles still floating in the air at suppertime, the village takes on green hues. When the purple has finally faded from Hunger Hill and the ditchwater colours are trying to sort themselves into the children's paint-boxes for the night, the cats appear. They walk in a dim spectrum on the fences down by the pit head, their fur slowly turning to shades of myrtle and olive, and one tom cat in particular sings love songs to his many mates; then he sprays the wood with the secretions from his sex glands. He heralds the night as surely as the cockerel foreshadows the day and the menfolk in our houses begin to fidget in their armchairs. And maybe once a year, coincidentally when the moon is full and casting opal beams into the scattering dust, even the dark stones of the terrace suddenly begin to sparkle like emeralds. It's then that those who are able take to their beds or to the bushes, wrap themselves tightly in their partners' arms and stay that way exploring and re-exploring orifice and mucosa until the dawn wakes them with a bang. The winding wheel squeaks, the semen hangs like spittle and the men dress for another day's toil. That's what they don't understand in London, that's what they have to come and see for themselves if ever they are to realise what a differing people we are.

In the years following the strike there were two such nights that I can recall. The first was soon after I had started working in the pit. I walked home with Billy. The moon was up. The furze growing about the rat-ridden land at the pit head was green as the grass, the cats screamed at one another, fur frozen on arched backs, and the stone twinkled at first like broken glass then with a fresh input of moondust, like freshly cut emeralds. And on the wires slung from chimney pot to gas lamp two exotic figures moved among the stars. Rosanne and Clarrie had returned to our village.

'What are they doin' 'ere?' Billy asked in a gruff voice which I ignored.

I stared at Clarrie a few feet above my head. She had taken on a new shape in her absence. She curved at the thigh and at the waist, she had developed breasts. I gazed at the pale full moon. It looked like a hole in the sky and I imagined that I could see clean through it. I then stared at the slumbering terrace of houses. There wasn't an electric light to be seen. Somewhere a lass giggled and I felt suddenly discomforted in my baggy trousers held at the middle with a bit of old cord.

'Doesn't tha naw?' I asked.

'Naw they's bloody hoss thieves,' Billy answered.

I looked about the common and heard the lass giggle again but this time from further away as if she'd somewhere been lifted into the sky.

'Better go back to H. G. Wells, Billy,' I advised my friend, knowing that the magic was not for him.

'Naw she nicked tha family's fortune,' Billy told me as he turned to go. He shouted good-night and ambled off to the terrace end and I heard him close the door. I looked up to the two figures on the wire. They knew that I was there watching them but they hadn't yet acknowledged me. They had ostrich feathers in their hair which took on the colour of the sea and their sequinned thighs shone a strange subdued silver. I sat in the rubber armchair and watched them for a time. They were the colour of pixies. Then without my knowing how she had got there, Rosanne was naked astride me and thrusting herself onto my erect penis. My trousers were about my ankles. Her young

162

daughter was removing my shirt and moving her tongue over my back and my nipples. The girl in the sky giggled from much further off than before. Then the three of us, naked, were walking as if we were pushing through water towards the wagon which was submerged only a short distance away. We lay wrapped together beneath a Mexican blanket until, like all the others who had succumbed to the magic of the green night, dawn woke us with a bang. I quietly left the wagon and went back towards the house, stopping to struggle up with the armchair which I carried with me and manoeuvred carefully through the door. From now on I was to sleep with Lancaster and Mr Brown in the parlour.

Nobody from the family was too pleased to see Rosanne and Ernest accused her directly of stealing the family fortune, but she denied it emphatically. Yes, in a moment of grief she had gone off with the plumed horses and she regretted it but she had never even had a sight of Great Great Grandmother's nest egg. As far as she was aware, Albert had dug up the suitcase from around the Roman wall on Hunger Hill and had immediately reburied it elsewhere for safe-keeping. When she was pressed by my father she admitted that Albert might have hidden it in the pit – which would explain how he came to be wearing Bresci's hat when he died. Ernest, my father and I then spent some time searching about the pit for Albert's new hiding place. Word soon got about and others joined in the search. Before long nobody was hewing coal any more, but everyone was digging in the most unlikely places in an attempt to find the missing money.

The brass was never uncovered though some amazing things were turned up in the scramble to find it. In the first instance, three more rubber women were found buried in the galleries, the last one causing a terrible fright as a collier put his pick through the doll's head. It produced an almighty explosion which most thought was due to fire damp and led to a panic in which Billy broke his leg. It seems that Elyahou Tsiblitz had sent his latest invention to a number of other bachelors besides our Lancaster. Then one day a stash of false teeth and rubber legs was found together with a whole sheaf of my aunt Henrietta's poetry. We could only conclude that she and Mr Tsiblitz had been down the pit one day to hide unwanted property but nobody could imagine when such an excursion had taken place. When the Ascot Gold Cup turned up nobody said anything. My father just took it into Leeds as he had done twenty years before but this time made certain that it was melted down. He put the money that he received for it into the miners' welfare fund.

The find which gave me the most pleasure, however, was the skeleton of a horse. It was found complete and wedged in a fissure leading off one of the galleries. It belonged to the massive shire horse which used to pull Rosanne's wagon – the one which had galloped off when it was brought into the pit because it had been frightened of the dark. Mr Brown and I took it up to the surface a bit at a time and rebuilt it, hitched in its harness in front of the wagon.

Then, because of all that extra digging in unlikely places, the pit roof began to crumble and it finally collapsed, killing two men. Everyone blamed Rosanne. If she hadn't returned to the village none of this would ever have happened. Billy, still with a broken leg, threw stones at the wagon and daubed slogans on the side suggesting that we were better off without the French. My father defended her for a time until Billy told him that I didn't always sleep in my armchair but sometimes was to be seen creeping across the common to spend the night in the arms of the two lasses. My father removed his belt and leathered me then he too threw stones at the wagon until one muddy morning, having had enough, Rosanne unhitched the skeleton horse and replaced it with a pit pony. She blew me a kiss,

164

Clarrie swore that she would love me to her death and they went away in the thin drizzle.

Throughout this time, of course, Jacky Jellis's voice had continued to boom from the walls of the New Royal Cinema. The nobs continued to pour in from London and my grandmother was approaching her second ton of fish head pie. Then one day nobody came. And nobody came the next day either. The wind of change was about to blow itself through the cinema on my land. *The Jazz Singer* had opened up in London. The cinema audience could see real talking pictures with real film stars now. Lancaster took his film spool home. Two weeks later he was on a boat bound for America. One might have understood if Mr Pinkofsky had been bitter but he showed no unkindness, he had no regrets. He had made his money just as Rube Hardwick and Emily Brightside had made theirs. They had made it whilst the talking picture had boomed. It was a blip in their careers. Just as the film itself had been a blip in the career of Lancaster Brightside – now he was on his way to America to show the world what a great film maker he could be.

Mr Brown's consumption got worse and he decided to leave the pit. He had a little tucked away, mostly earned from his winnings when betting against Bottom Boat Beauty. He continued to live in our house though. Then one day I saw my future come together with my past. I told George Smart to stick his stinking coal pit. I sat on the common with Mr Brown with the skeleton of a horse grazing before us. Between its ribs we could see the pit and the cinema at Hunger Hill. The wind whistled through the old bones causing doors to bang.

'All them seats,' I said. 'It's like a bloody church.'

'Nay, it's nowt like a church, lad. Tha doesn't want to 'ave owt to do with that stuff.'

'Well, it's like a museum then.'

'Ay. It'll be like a museum,' he said. 'Take out them seats and it'll be just like a museum.'

I was squinting between the horse's bones. Marvelling at the way one could see the cinema right through where the flesh had been, and suddenly the bones and the building were one. The skeleton was inside the fabric of the building.

'How long did it take to put that thing together?' I asked.

'About six weeks, I think. Must've been a bloody record.'

'No. Not the cinema. The horse. How long did it take to build the skeleton?'

'A week maybe. Don't really remember.'

'And how long does tha think it'll take to put the dinosaur together?'

'A year perhaps.'

'Ay. That's what I was thinking.'

'Come on, lad,' said Mr Brown. 'Let's go and see.' He stood up and spat a black gobbet of muck into the ground.

Gradually throughout the next year we cleared the cinema of its seats and brought the bones from the disused pit. We borrowed books from the libraries and made a trip to the Natural History Museum in London to see the iguanodons. Slowly we put the skeleton together inside the building and we had expert palaeontologists come to view it. Nobody said anything but we knew that it couldn't have been quite right. My great grandfather's bones were in there somewhere but it didn't matter – the skeleton looked just like the pictures in the books.

Mr Brown had Jacky Jellis impersonate a dinosaur's roar and when he played it over Movietone it sounded to be the most ferocious thing that anyone had ever heard. Here was my museum. The schools brought their children from far and wide to see the only complete dinosaur skeleton in the North of England and to hear the only authentic dinosaur roar that was left in the whole of the world.

15

How Mr Brown came to lead the blind

The Jam Sahib's motor was a twenty-eight horsepower Lanchester which had been built in about 1907. It was a massive vehicle and could accommodate ten persons quite comfortably. My great great grandmother had bought it from Elyahou Tsiblitz soon after it had been built. Since almost the first week of its being in our family my father had taken the less privileged in the car, on trips to places where they might breathe more easily and look at hills and rivers without having to see them through the filter of coal dust which nearly always hung in the village air. Such trips for these people had been the dearest wish of my great great grandmother and there was talk at the time that it was the sole reason for her purchase.

One bright red morning, my father asked Mr Brown if he would drive the blinded up into the dales as had been promised them. Unfortunately my father had come down with the chickenpox and was unable to go. Mr Brown agreed that he would stand in for my father and asked me if I would like to accompany him on the trip as he was uncertain that he could handle all of those blind people on his own. At that time Mr Brown and I looked after the museum together but after discussion we decided not to open up for that day, packed our sandwiches and set off in the motor with half a dozen men who couldn't see the end of a nose between them. Mr Brown took the car through Ilkley and Skipton to Settle where he turned off the main road and followed a path to the foot of a mountain.

'That's Pen-y-ghent,' our lodger told me. I looked at the

sunny hill and was immediately reminded of a loaf brown-
ing in the oven. 'We'll tek 'em up that path,' he said.

'What, tha means tha's going to tek this lot up there?'

'Ay. Why not?'

'But they're blind, Mr Brown,' I confided, trying to keep
my voice down.

'That's nowt,' he said. 'Come on. Give us a hand.'

We helped the men from the motor and had them sit in a
circle on the grass, then Mr Brown lifted out the back seat
and produced an enormous coil of rope.

'Now, we're off for a little walk up this 'ere 'ill,' he told
the men on the grass. 'Don't tha worry 'bout nowt. There's
a rope.'

'Will we 'ave to tie it round us middles?' asked a man who
had no eyes and who until this moment thought that he
had banished mountain climbing from his list of allowed
activities.

Mr Brown stared at the empty sockets for a moment and
said, 'No. Nowt like that. Rope's fixed. Tha just feel for
t'rope. It goes from 'ere right the way to top. It'll be like
walking up steps with tha hand on a banister rail.' Then he
helped the man up and made him hold the rope for a few
seconds. 'Can tha feel it?' he asked.

'Ay.'

'Well, it's a bit slack just 'ere but tha'll get more confidence further up the hill where it tightens up a bit.'

I took our lodger to one side and said, 'Mr Brown, tha
can't be serious about this. They'll never mek it to the top.
They'll never mek it fifty yards without falling over the
edge.'

'It'll be all right, lad, tha'll see,' he tried assuring me.

'But Mr Brown, I don't like this. It's having a bit of fun at
their expense. It's not right.'

'Fun, lad, tha calls it fun? It's not fun, lad. It's deadly
serious is this. It's giving these people back their self-respect is this. It's not fun. Nobody will be laughing, lad, least
of all yours truly. Now come on, get thasen moving, we

don't want to be bringing them down in the dark.' He started to cough and I watched this man who was already talking about bringing half a dozen blind men down a mountain even before we had got them up there, and God alone knew how we were going to achieve that. I watched the muck coughed from his lungs as it caught in the wind-whipped blades of grass. It nestled there like cuckoo spit. 'Now, tha get hold of back end of rope and I'll tek lead,' he said. 'And for God's sake keep it taut.'

'I thought tha didn't believe in God?' I chided, unable to disguise the sneer in my voice.

'Not believe? I never said owt like that, lad. I believe all right. Believe more than most,' he told me. 'Just can't stand all this prayin' and praisin', that's all. God don't listen, lad, and why should he, so what's the point in talkin' and singin' to him?' He looked over to the six blind men. 'Ask them,' he said. 'Ask them how much he listens.' I watched a lark twittering high above the summit of the hill. 'Too busy, lad. Too busy to listen to all that stuff is God. But he's there all right. I believe that. Anyroad, who the fuck do you think is going to get us up to the top of this 'ere mountain, eh?' I couldn't reply as I struggled with such an irrational chastisement. 'Come on, get a hold of the rope end and like I said keep it taut.'

'I'll keep it taut, Mr Brown, tha worry about t'other end,' and I sniffed back a tear.

'Good lad,' he said, then he led the blind men one at a time and stood them, spaced several yards apart from each other, on the right hand side of the rope telling each one not to move. Our lodger then went to the head of the line which he had formed, picked up the other end of the rope, slung it over his shoulder and set off up the hill tugging it tight.

'Right, stick out tha left hands,' he called, then after a moment he asked, ''As tha got it? 'As tha got the rope?' From where I was at the rear of the line I could see that each man had a grip on the rope and I called up that everyone had got a hold on the rope. 'Right, keep on walking and

169

keep on feeling for the rope. Like I said it goes right to the bloody top so there's no need to worry.' Then he turned round and shouted, 'And for God's sake keep tha bloody feet up. Lift tha knees and tha'll 'ave nowt to worry about, does thee understand?'

'Ay,' all the blind men chorused and we set off at a slow march up the path which would take us all the way to the summit. After we had gone about fifteen yards the six men started to bunch up towards Mr Brown who then shouted for us to stop exactly where we were. He instructed the men to leave go of the rope, something which they were hesitant in doing.

'Trust me,' he shouted, 'and if tha can't trust me then trust in God, all right?' The men let go of the rope. He then walked about fifteen to twenty yards up the path taking the rope and I at the end of it with him and causing me almost to bump into the man at the back of the line. Then he shouted, 'Right, stick out tha left hands again,' and once more the group of men took up the rope and walked a little further towards the peak. In this stop and start fashion and with several stumbles along the way the men climbed to the top of Pen-y-ghent.

We sat about the cairn and ate our sandwiches and Mr Brown told the men how he could see the sea in directions both east and west. He said that he could see the seagulls flying over Scarborough and told them how he could see the anglers who were landing dolphins and sharks from off the pier at Blackpool. And when one of the men asked me if Mr Brown was right and was it possible to really see such things I remained silent for ages pretending not to have heard the question until a bird's feather came spinning out of the sky and landed on my jam sandwich shaft first, and as I picked it off and put the feather in my pocket I said, 'Ay. Of course it is. True as God's my judge, there's dolphins and sharks and there's a man riding out to sea on the back of a turtle.' And the blind man smiled and told us all that this was the best day of his life and of how he'd always

170

believed that one day he would marry a mermaid, at which news Mr Brown couldn't stop laughing. Not until it was time to come down the mountain.

'Right,' he shouted. 'We'll be turning round, remember, so tha'll be needing to hold the rope with tha right hands this time. Is that all right? Is there anyone who isn't comfy with the thought of changing hands?'

'I'm not,' said the man with no eyes. 'I've got arthritis in my right hand. I'll not grip right.'

'Well, that's no problem,' Mr Brown told him and went through the charade of passing the man under the rope and have him grip it with his left hand. Then we came down the mountain in the same fashion as we had gone up it.

I don't think that anyone knows why Wenceslas Piggott's motor was never removed from the crossroads after he had the accident. But it never was. A family of mice had made their home from the upholstery on the front passenger seat, and what they didn't live in they lived on. They had eaten most of it. A family of thrushes had made their nest in the driving seat and the back seat was given over to various activities. The young ones, during the day, used it as a hiding place or as a place for setting up house. The older ones did a spot of courting in the back at night but until Mr Brown drove the Jam Sahib's motor into the back of it nobody had any idea that the policeman ate his sandwiches there too. It was one of those nights when the world turns sparkling green and how Mr Brown didn't see it I shall never know but there you are, he didn't, and the policeman who had just climbed into the back of the stationary motor and was about to start on his cold bacon sandwich was given a real jolt.

Oddly enough, one of the blind men said that he saw Marlene Jellis standing in the road just before the accident and that gave everybody the creeps. It also initiated a whole set of new rumours – there were many prepared to believe in the ghost of Marlene Jellis. It was put about that she wasn't living with Sosthenes Smith after all, that there had been collusion between Archie and Mr Piggott, though nobody could imagine why. Perhaps Archie had just become one of those wishy-washy liberal doctors who saw murderers as being sick in the head and in need of care. That's why he's in the asylum, they said. But it was spooky, wasn't it? Who better than a blind man to see a ghost up at the spot where the woman's clothes were known to have been found? The poor soul was only looking for her bloomers, Mrs Gill told my grandmother.

The policeman was badly shaken, having his back banged like that, but at least he was on hand when we had calmed him sufficiently to investigate the accident and make a few notes with his blue pencil.

Mr Willmott sat in our parlour and brought a fart from the direction of my grandmother who, when all eyes fell upon her, reddened considerably. She looked at the corpse on the table hoping that some of us at least might think the noise had come from there. Mr Willmott remained impassive, his long black tash hiding his ventriloquist lips. He too looked at the corpse, thinking that perhaps he had not thrown his voice far enough. Mr Brown, dressed in his Sunday suit, was the third corpse which I had seen. The first, that of my great great grandmother, had appeared to be very dead. She looked like a pickled walnut despite the fact that Emily had washed the coal dust from her skin. I tell you, she was like a pickled walnut. That of my uncle Albert had seemed to be asleep. Mr Brown, though, looked to be wide awake. His alert blue eyes were open, drinking in the surrounding room despite the fact that there was a hole right through his middle where the steering column had penetrated. The room itself was quiet and appeared to be the dead thing in our midst. I looked about me at the others present. The parson, my grandfather, my parents – they

were unmoving. Mr Brown's blue eyes and my grandmother's red cheeks – at that moment it was they who gave
our parlour its liveliness. My father and the parson put him
in a coffin and nailed down the lid after throwing in our
lodger's extra collar stud. We took him to the crematorium
in Wakefield and Mr Willmott remained outside watching
over his plumed horses. He didn't want a repetition of what
happened on the last occasion our family had to draw on
the services of the Burial Society.

My grandfather stood up and made a short speech explaining how it was only fitting that a man like Brown
should be cremated for he claimed that cremation somehow went along with the man's anonymity. He came from
nowhere and nobody knew very much about him. We'll
scatter the ashes, he told the small congregation, and send
him back to wherever he arrived from – that's about the best
we can do for the man.

'There's more to it than that, grandfather,' I said, 'he had
a spirit did Mr Brown, a real spirit. Cremation will release
that much from the old bones. His spirit will find its way
back to where it needs to be. That's why he preferred
cremation, he didn't want that spirit locked in no more, and
as for the ashes, well, if nobody objects I think I would
rather keep them at the museum. He doesn't need no
scattering.'

Nobody seemed to object so I took the urn back to the
village and set it on a plinth next to the iguanodon. He had
been the last of the dossing colliers which my family had
known. There were no others after Mr Brown. If, as I have
said before, Bill Pettit was born before his time then I reckon
that Mr Brown had come in right on cue. He made up his
life on the run, so to speak, and he painted us like he
wanted, right into his own and the world's fabric of being.
After his funeral my father took the wide winged chairs
from our parlour and burned them on the common. He
bought a couch which converted at night into a bed and for
a time that's where I laid my head.